ABOUT THE AUTHORS

USA TODAY bestselling author **Kimberly Raye** started her first novel in high school and has been writing ever since. To date, she's published more than fifty-eight novels, two of them prestigious RITA® Award nominees. She's also been nominated by *RT Book Reviews* for several Reviewer's Choice awards, as well as a career achievement award. Kim lives deep in the heart of Texas Hill Country with her husband and their young children. She's an avid reader who loves Diet Dr Pepper, Facebook, chocolate and alpha males. Kim also loves to hear from readers. You can visit her online at www.kimberlyraye.com or follow her on Twitter.

Over the course of her career, *New York Times* and *USA TODAY* bestselling author **Julie Leto** has published more than forty books—all of them sexy and all of them romances at heart. She shares a popular blog—www.plotmonkeys.com—with her best friends Carly Phillips, Janelle Denison and Leslie Kelly, and would love for you to follow her on Twitter, where she goes by @JulieLeto. She's a born-and-bred Floridian homeschooling mom with a love for her family, her friends, her dachshund, her lynx-point Siamese and supersexy stories with a guaranteed happy ending.

Kimberly Raye
Julie Leto

BLAZING BEDTIME STORIES,
VOLUME VIII

HARLEQUIN®
entertain, enrich, inspire™

ISBN-13: 978-0-373-79704-2

BLAZING BEDTIME STORIES, VOLUME VIII

Copyright © 2012 by Harlequin Books S.A.

The publisher acknowledges the
copyright holders of the individual works
as follows:

THE COWBOY WHO NEVER GREW UP
Copyright © 2012 by Kimberly Raye Groff

HOOKED
Copyright © 2012 by Book Goddess, LLC

Recycling programs
for this product may
not exist in your area.

CONTENTS

KIMBERLY RAYE

THE COWBOY
WHO NEVER GREW UP

For my oldest son, Josh,
who is growing up way too fast!

I'm so proud of you.

And for the supertalented Julie Leto,
It was great working with you on this story.

I knew you had a little Texas in you!

1

HE WAS THE PERFECT COWBOY for the job.

Wendy Darlington stared at the man who slid off the angry bull in the middle of the massive rodeo arena in Fort Worth, Texas, and her breath caught. Dust exploded. The crowd roared. The animal twisted and turned as the wranglers tried to get him under control, but the rider wasn't the least bit nervous. He sidestepped her and headed for the dusty Stetson he'd lost during the most amazing ride Wendy had ever seen. Eight seconds and then some. The buzzer had come and gone, but Pete Gunner had kept at it until he'd snagged bragging rights to breaking yet another world record.

He parked the cowboy hat back on his head and flashed a grin before heading toward the gate and the cluster of reporters waiting to swallow him up.

The scores went up and, sure enough, they were high enough to push Pete into first and solidify a place in the upcoming Professional Bull Riders finals.

Not that she'd had any doubt.

Pete Gunner was the best of the best. An eight-time PBR champion and record holder on the fast track to win number nine.

Unfortunately he had a weakness for loud parties and lots of women, and so he was even more notorious for his behavior outside of the arena. He was a wild child. Unpredictable. Uncensored. Unmanageable.

Trouble. Big, *big* trouble.

That's what Wendy had told her boss when he'd come up with the crazy idea of making Pete Gunner the newest spokesperson for Western America, the biggest leatherworks company in the Southwest. They made everything from custom cowboy boots and specialty chaps to one-of-a-kind hand-tooled saddles. The company was launched during the late seventies at the height of the *Urban Cowboy* craze, with their products targeted toward the sophisticated, professional types eager to jump on the chuck wagon and play weekend cowboy.

They'd managed to maintain a decent profit share over the years, too, although their early heyday had long since faded with so many competitors flooding the marketplace.

Wendy had come to Western straight out of college as an intern and had slowly worked her way up from administrative aide to senior marketing representative. She'd put in nine years at the company and managed to keep up sales in an economic downturn. She'd fought tooth and nail to make a name for herself within the company, and she deserved to be moved up for it. She'd even told her boss, Fred, as much when she'd asked for a promotion last year.

But the man didn't want to maintain his company's position. He wanted to sell the company for a hefty profit and buy his own private island in the Bahamas. Something that wasn't going to happen, at least for the kind of money he wanted, if he didn't get his market share up by twenty percent.

At least that's what a private-business consultant had told him six months ago. Hence the creation of Outlaw Outfitters, a line of modestly priced products geared toward the younger segment, and the brainstorm to have Pete Gunner as the front man.

A real cowboy backing the new line would up its credibility and get the attention of the multitude of younger rodeo fans. As the senior marketing rep, it was Wendy's job to make it happen. Or else.

Those had been Fred's exact words.

Make this happen and I'll make sure you stay on with the company after I sell. Or else you can find a new job.

Which meant moving on, starting over.

The story of Wendy's life.

Growing up the only child of single parent and baseball legend Mitch Darlington, Wendy had become an expert in *new*. During her childhood, she'd spent the season headed to a new city every week and the off-season living in a condo near the training camp for whatever team her dad had been signed with at the time. Thanks to a huge ego and a know-it-all attitude, he'd been traded eleven times over a fifteen-year period, during which Wendy had zigzagged across the country with him. She'd even lived in Toronto for six months while he'd played with the Toronto Blue Jays.

No more.

The moment she'd graduated college, she'd promised herself that her days of moving from place to place were officially over. She'd accepted the job at Western America, bought a house in Houston, and she'd been settled ever since. She'd made friends and built a life for herself. And while the actual day-to-day could be boring at times, she still preferred it hands down to the nomadic lifestyle she'd grown up with.

She wasn't losing her job.

Fred wanted Pete's signature on the multimillion-dollar endorsement package her company had offered, and Wendy was going to make it happen. Mr. Wild and Reckless had already given them a verbal agreement months ago, but it had been one mishap after the other when it came to getting him to actually sign. They'd overnighted the initial documents as was policy, but then he'd claimed his dog had chewed them up. He'd left set number two in a hotel room in Vegas. Number three had ended up at the bottom of a bull pen. Number four had disappeared in a truck stop somewhere between Nashville and New Mexico.

While Wendy had freaked over each "accident," Pete had laughed them off as just another day in the life of PBR's most notorious cowboy.

Don't get your panties in a wad, darlin'. That's what he'd told her on the phone in the deepest, sexiest drawl she'd ever heard. *Just send out another set.*

Not this time.

Numbers five and six—she'd brought an extra—were safe and sound in her briefcase and she wasn't leaving until everything was signed.

Or else...

She fought down a wave of anxiety, popped an antacid from the roll in her pocket and steeled herself. Briefcase in hand, she made her way around the arena wall until she reached the cluster of bull pens. A security guard stopped her in her tracks, but she flashed a VIP pass at him and he waved her forward. She was just about to turn a corner and head for the excitement when she barreled into the hard wall of a very muscular chest.

Her head snapped up and she found herself staring at her worst marketing nightmare.

She'd seen plenty of pictures of Pete Gunner over the past few months: everything from professional publicity shots of him climbing into a saddle or dusting himself off after a grueling ride, to a papparazzi's wet dream where he'd been table-dancing at Billy Bob's honkytonk or lapping at a watering trough after the PBR finals in Vegas.

But nothing in print could begin to compare with the man himself.

Several day's growth of stubble shadowed his jaw and circled his sensuous mouth. Whiskey-colored hair framed his rugged face and brushed the collar of his white button-down shirt. Vivid blue eyes peered at her from beneath the brim of a beat-up Stetson.

"Don't be in such a hurry, sugar." He gave her his infamous grin, his lips crooked just a hint at the corner, and her heart did a double *thump*. "It's always better if you take your time."

Not that Wendy was the least bit attracted. She knew his type all too well. She'd grown up with such a man, and while she loved her dad, she wasn't falling for a man just like him. She liked her men stable. Controlled. Reliable.

She drew a deep breath and ignored the fluttering in her chest.

"I—" The rest of her words stalled in a choked cough as the antacid took a nosedive down the wrong pipe.

His eyebrows drew together. "You okay, sugar?"

"I—" She swallowed. "I—I'm fine," she finally managed to say.

He grinned and her heart started again. Her hands trembled and her tummy tingled.

Seriously?

He was just a man. Sure, he was sexier than most

with his bad-boy drawl and seductive smile, but still…
She wasn't going to let that turn her to a pile of quivering Jell-O, even if she had been so busy with the new Outlaw line that she'd had zero time for a social life over the past six months. Her self-imposed celibacy was *not* going to jump up and bite her during the most important ten seconds of her career.

She stiffened and gathered her control. "You're just the person I wanted to see. I need you to sign—"

"There's plenty of signed photos at the press table," he cut in. "You can take your pick."

"No, no." She shook her head. "I don't want a signed picture."

"A body signature?" His eyes darkened with a look of pure, raw passion and her mouth went dry again. "Above the waist or below?"

She licked her lips and tried to ignore the way his eyes followed the movement. "No, of course not. I've got these papers for you—"

"Pete!" The shout came from her right and she turned to find a burly cowboy motioning him forward. "Giddyup, dude. We've got to get the hell out of here!"

"I hate to cut this short, but I've got someplace I really need to be." And just like that, he turned and walked away.

Wendy watched the push and pull of his Wranglers as he disappeared into the crowd. He really did have a great butt. She could totally see why every woman in the eighteen-to-forty-eight-year-old demographic was head over heels for him. The front view had been good, but the back was about the best she'd ever seen—

Hello?

He's walking away, remember? Which is what you'll

be doing when Fred finds out that you let him slip through your fingers.

She bolted forward and raced after him as if her life depended on it.

It did.

Her job, her home, her stability meant everything to her and she wasn't going to let some party-hearty cowboy screw it all up.

She was getting that signature, no matter what she had to do.

2

THERE WAS A NAKED WOMAN in his bed.

Pete Gunner came to that conclusion the moment he yanked aside the curtains leading to the rear of the sleek black tour bus.

The woman sat up. Dark brown hair spilled down around her shoulders. Excitement fired her gaze. The sheet fell to her waist. Yep, she was naked, all right.

As an eight-time PBR champion and the circuit's reigning wild child, it was a scene he was all too familiar with. Buckle bunnies were par for the course. And bare-assed buckle bunnies? An added bonus.

If it had been any other night.

"It's really you, isn't it?" she murmured. "*The* Pete Gunner."

"So they say."

Her gaze narrowed for a split second. "You look different than you do in your poster." She licked her full lips. "Better. Much better."

He tipped his hat and gave her the famous Gunner Grin. "You're not so bad yourself." And then he did the one thing he would never have done if it had been any other night. He took a step forward and retrieved her tank top and jeans that were draped across a nearby chair. "As much as I'd like to take you up on the offer, I'm afraid now isn't a good time." He set her clothes on the edge of the bed. "Why don't you get dressed and I'll get my bus driver to fetch an autographed picture and a few rodeo passes for you?"

A pout tugged at her lush bottom lip. "But I've been waiting all this time for you." She pushed up on her knees and the sheet fell to the bed. "I thought we could have a little fun. You do like to have fun, don't you?"

Hell, yeah. Fun was his motto. He'd been wild and reckless from the get-go, hitting the rodeo circuit hard at the age of seventeen, and the local bars even harder after that. He lived to cut loose and live it up. Damn straight, he did.

At the same time, it was already *this* close to midnight and he was more than six hours away from home. That meant he would be on the road all night if he intended to reach Lost Gun by sunup.

He'd figured on leaving right after he'd run into that pretty little blonde wanting his autograph on a certain body part. Hell, he hadn't even had the chance to imagine which part—her luscious breast or maybe one rounded hip or a tight ass cheek—before he'd been sideswiped by several Wrangler reps wanting to talk to him about yet another endorsement. They'd wasted over an hour and so now he was really pressed. That, and his back was aching something fierce. Jasper, one of the meanest bulls this side of the Rio Grande, had thrown him pretty hard after that last buzzer.

Not that a few aches and pains would have held him back from having some fun with his new bed partner. *Hell,* no. He would have ripped his clothes off in a heartbeat if tonight had been like any other.

But it wasn't. His kid brother was counting on him to make it back to West Texas for his eighteenth birthday, and so time was of the essence.

"Thanks for the offer, sugar, but I'll have to take a rain check."

"What about that autograph?" Her voice followed him as he turned.

"Get dressed," he called over his shoulder. "And it'll be my pleasure."

He started toward the front of the bus. He was halfway there when a different woman stepped out of the bathroom, a redhead with brown eyes and an interested smile. She wore a leather halter top, a miniskirt and a come-and-get-me-cowboy expression. She blocked his path and waved a Sharpie at him.

"I've been waiting for you—" She started the same spiel he'd heard after every rodeo since he'd won his first bull riding championship twelve years ago. She was ready and willing and able to do whatever he wanted, for as long as he wanted. In return for bragging rights and the ever-popular autograph, that is. He'd scribbled his signature on too many places to count—a hand, a thigh, a breast, a butt cheek. He'd even done matching autographs for the Dallas Cowboy Cheerleaders last year—left shoulder blade. Except for that one cheerleader. They'd needed someplace a lot more private than Cowboys Stadium for what she'd had in mind. And, being the ever-obliging cowboy, he'd gone out of his way to make her happy.

Then and now, he reminded himself. Even if the only thing he wanted to do at the moment was ice down his shoulder and pop a few Tylenols.

"—thought maybe you and I could get acquainted,"

she went on. "I've been a fan for years and there's nothing I wouldn't do—"

"That's great, sugar," he cut in, giving her his infamous smile, "but I'll have to take a rain check." He sidestepped her and left her staring after him.

He wasn't trying to be rude. Hell, he loved women. All women. Brunettes. Redheads. Blondes.

Especially blondes with green eyes.

His thoughts torpedoed back to the arena and the woman he'd stumbled into earlier. She'd been all stuffed up with her button-up blouse and stiff black skirt, her hair pulled back into a no-nonsense ponytail. Nothing like most of the buckle bunnies who hung out near the chutes. Then again, he'd learned never to judge a long time ago and so he knew the hands-off vibe he'd gotten off her had been just an act. Obviously a damned good one since he was still thinking about her. And her luscious body. And her eyes. She'd had the prettiest he'd ever seen. Rich. Potent. Mesmerizing. Like ripe pastureland after a month of April showers.

Her image haunted him for a few more heartbeats before he managed to tuck it away and focus on the situation at hand.

Women.

Yep, he loved 'em and he never failed to make time. And he sure as hell didn't mind signing autographs for each and every one. He loved his fans.

But this was different. It was crunch time. His younger brother's birthday was tomorrow and Pete intended to be there when Wade rolled out of bed. He'd never let the kid down before and he sure as shootin' wasn't going to start now. Wade had seen enough disappointment in his young life. They both had.

"Don't tell me," Eli McGinnis said when Pete stepped

off the bus and found him standing nearby. "One got past me." Eli had a head full of steel-gray hair and a mustache to match. He wore a straw cowboy hat, a pearl-snap shirt and a pair of starched Wranglers. Word on the circuit had it that he was seventy-five if he was a day, but to hear Eli tell it he was barely legal. "Dammit to hell, I hate a crafty gal."

"It was two gals," Pete told his driver. "Aren't you supposed to be standing guard until we're ready to pull out?"

"I cain't be standing around all day babysitting this big old bus like I ain't got nothin' better to do."

"That's what I pay you for." Eli had been working for Pete ever since the man had retired from the rodeo circuit himself. Pete had learned the ropes from Eli, so he owed him. He'd given him a job and a place to live after he'd retired. Eli had been a permanent fixture in his life ever since.

"You pay me to drive," Eli reminded him. "Besides, you ain't the only rooster in the bunch, you know." He tugged at his pants and straightened his belt buckle. "Maybe I had a little female company that I just couldn't turn down. A man like me's got needs, ya know."

Pete eyed him. "Bathroom break?" he finally asked.

"Funnel cake." Eli swiped at the powdered sugar that clung to the corner of his mustache. "But just so's you know, I surely ain't lost my touch. That there cake was served up by a mighty nice-looking female named Justine." He grinned. "Why, she gave me a few extra shakes of sugar and didn't even charge me for 'em."

Before Pete could point out that Justine gave everybody extra shakes because she had a nervous condition that made her hands tremble, his two stowaways came sashaying off the bus. Pete spent the next few minutes signing two autographs—left shoulder blade and right bikini line—and posing for some quick pictures before managing to excuse himself and disappear back inside.

"Are they gone?" he asked when Eli finally climbed back inside the bus and powered the door shut behind him.

"For now, but I wouldn't go counting my chickens just yet. One of them twittered or tweedled or some such nonsense and I saw a whole mess of females coming around the semi parked just behind us." He shook his head. "Which means we'd better get the hell out of here 'afore somebody else crawls up in here. It's a helluva long way home." Eli climbed behind the wheel and radioed security to clear a path.

A few seconds later, the bus rumbled forward and Pete breathed a sigh of relief.

Followed by a growl of aggravation when he walked into the bathroom a few minutes later and pulled back the shower curtain. And found yet another woman waiting for him.

The woman.

The stiff, conservative blonde with the pretty green eyes.

As irritated as he was, there was just something about the way she stared up at him that made him smile. Oddly enough, the fatigue slipped away and excitement rippled up his spine. "Determined to get that autograph, are you?"

She was the one to smile this time. A light sparked in her incredible green eyes and his heart skipped a beat. "You have no idea."

3

"So where do you want it?" Pete Gunner's deep, sexy voice slid into her ears, skimmed along her nerve endings, and for a split second, Wendy forgot all about her job.

Her brain conjured a quick visual of his fingers working at the buttons of her blouse and his rough palm grazing her breast as he branded her with his touch.

She stiffened and reached for her briefcase. "Right here." She pulled out the stack of papers and slapped them into his palm before she did something really stupid.

Like give in to the sudden heat slip-sliding up and down her spine, then rip off her clothes and press herself up against his hard, hot body.

Besides, she'd meant *no matter what* as in chasing him down and hiding out in his bus and cornering him when he had no easy means of escape. Not jumping him.

Not yet.

She ignored her crying hormones and steeled herself. "Just sign these and I'll be out of your hair."

He stared at the contract, his gaze drinking in the

first page before colliding with hers. Surprise glittered in his bright blue eyes. "You're from Western America?"

"Wendy Darlington. Marketing." She held out her hand to shake, but he just kept staring at her as if she'd grown two heads.

"Darlington," he murmured, seeming to turn the name over in his mind. "Wasn't there a pitcher by the name of Mitch Darlington?"

"Daddy dearest."

"No way."

"Way. Now can we—"

"Say, didn't he pitch for the Texas Rangers at one time?"

"And the Cubs and the Red Sox and a handful of others that have nothing to do with why I'm here. You agreed to sign and I'm here to make sure that happens." She motioned to the documents in his hand. "There's only one signature line on the last page, but there are several spots that you need to initial in between. Those are all marked." She pulled out a pen and handed it to him. "Just sign it all and I'll be out of your way. You can drop me at the next intersection."

He seemed to contemplate her words for the next few moments while her heart beat a frantic rhythm. As if she feared he might refuse.

He wouldn't. He couldn't. They had a verbal agreement and that was as good as gold. This was just a formality.

A formality that would keep her from getting canned.

"It's nothing you haven't seen before," she rushed on. "No surprises. The money's all there. The terms are exactly what our lawyer spelled out."

"Sounds good. I'll get right on this." An easy grin

spread across his face. "Just as soon as I get cleaned up first."

"You could just sign it now and be done with it."

"You wouldn't want me to sign something I haven't read, now would you?"

"Of course not."

"Then it'll have to wait until after I take a shower."

The words conjured an image of his hard, rippled, naked body. Water sluiced over him, running in rivulets down his golden skin—

Um, excuse me. You're here to work, not fantasize.

Especially since Pete Gunner wasn't even close to her fantasy man. She liked calm, mild-mannered, understated men. Like Jim. He was the staff accountant for Western and he made an amazing lasagna. He'd brought it to the last office party and everyone had *ooh*ed and *ah*ed. He'd also invited her out a half-dozen times over the past year. Not that she'd accepted. She'd been so worried over the new line and Pete's role as spokesman that she hadn't wanted to spare the time.

That, and Jim was just about the most boring man she'd ever met.

She squelched the thought as soon as it struck.

Boring was good. Preferable to the love-'em-and-leave-'em type.

Then why are you standing here watching rodeo's biggest womanizer take off his shirt?

Pete undid the last button of his shirt and reality smacked her. "W-what are you doing?"

"Taking a shower, remember?" He grinned and the shirt dropped to the floor, revealing a muscular chest sprinkled with silky hair. "Unless you plan on washing my back, I'd get while the getting is good." He reached for the button on his jeans and she whirled. His laughter followed her out of the bathroom and into the living area of the bus.

A table stood to her left with a bench on one side and two plush-looking chairs on the other. She slid into one of the overstuffed chairs, plopped the papers down on the marble-topped table and drew a steadying breath.

Okay, so she'd had temporary brain malfunction. No big deal. She would simply reboot.

Pulling out a pen, she set everything out and flipped the page to the first spot he needed to initial. There. The moment Pete Gunner finished his precious shower, he would sign and she would head back to Houston.

Her job would be secure. Her life would be back on track. And she could finally breathe again.

Shifting her attention from the anxiety rippling in her stomach, she took a good long look at her surroundings. The motor coach was top-of-the-line with a rear bedroom, a full-size bathroom and a kitchen. A media center sat just to her left complete with a plasma TV, Blu-ray player and several other pieces of equipment that she couldn't identify. And then there was her chair.

The softest, most supple leather she'd ever felt. It tugged at her backside, cushioning her tired muscles, lulling her to sink back. Relax.

Not.

She perched on the edge, fully alert, ready for the handsome cowboy to waltz out of the bathroom so she could save her ass.

At least that was the plan for the first five minutes. But then five turned to ten and ten to twenty, and her back started to ache. She braced herself, but it only made her more uncomfortable. Maybe it wouldn't hurt to scoot back just a little. There. That was better.

It's not like she needed to be ready for a foot chase.

She had him cornered. If he wanted to stall, fine. She would kick back and wait him out.

The bus rolled along and the hum of the shower echoed in her ears. Before she knew what was happening, her head started to feel heavy. She slumped forward once, twice. She jerked upright and glanced at her watch. Ugh. It was half-past midnight and she'd been up since six in the morning. To make matters worse, she'd been tossing and turning every night for the past six months thanks to a certain unreliable cowboy. With her job hanging in the balance, sleep hadn't been a luxury she could afford. Not then and certainly not now.

She *had* to do this.

She yawned and fought to keep her eyes open. A battle she was destined to lose. The chair was too comfortable and the cowboy too damned slow, and suddenly there seemed nothing wrong with closing her eyes for just one teeny, tiny minute. Just to pass the time.

WHAT THE HELL was she doing here?

The thought echoed in Pete's head as he stood under the shower and let the hot water beat down on his sore muscles.

Okay, so he knew what she was doing here. Western had been dogging him with those contracts for months now and they'd obviously gotten tired of waiting. He couldn't blame them. They'd offered him one hell of a deal. One he'd be crazy to turn down. He would make more in one year as the Outlaw Outfitters spokesman than he'd made in the past three seasons on the circuit. Sure, it wasn't nearly as much fun. But at least it didn't hurt like hell.

He flexed his throbbing shoulder and tried to ignore the stab of pain that shot through him.

Signing was the best thing for him. He *knew* that.

Then stop fooling around and sign already.

He would.

He would haul his ass out there, read through everything, sign on the dotted line for the sexy little marketing exec who'd cornered him on his own bus, and be done with it.

With her.

At least that's what he told himself when he finally climbed out of the shower, dried off and put on a pair of clean jeans.

He found her slumped in a chair, her eyes closed, her lips parted. A steady snore filtered through the air and a smile touched his lips. She was a little thing, but she sure could belt one out.

He didn't blame her. He'd paid an arm and a leg for those chairs and he'd dozed off in them too many times to count. Particularly after a night like tonight.

He sank down in the chair nearest her and shifted his attention to the papers spread out on the table. Snatching up the copy, he kicked back and turned to the first page.

He meant to read the entire thing.

He really did.

But his shoulder nagged at him and he couldn't seem to concentrate. After two pages, he tossed the stack onto the table and reached for the remote control. A click of a button and a rerun of the latest NASCAR race blazed across the massive screen. The sound roared through the bus and she stirred.

With the fast reflexes of an eight-time PBR champion, Pete hit the mute button. The sound faded into the steady hum of the engine.

Wendy shifted, but she didn't open her eyes. Instead, she half turned, snuggling deeper into the chair.

He fixed his gaze on the TV and tried to ignore his throbbing muscles keeping tempo with his heartbeat. He could kiss a good night's sleep goodbye. Times like this, it was all he could do not to grind his teeth. Which was why he'd turned down the woman tucked into his bed. And the one stowed away in his bathroom. Even a warm, willing body wasn't enough to distract him from the pain wrenching through him after a particularly grueling ride.

But damned if the steady, hypnotic sound of Wendy Darlington's snoring didn't do just that as he sat there and the minutes ticked by. That, and she smelled really good. Like homemade peach ice cream. And heaven knew he'd always had a hankerin' for peaches.

He closed his eyes and focused on the soft *zzzzzzz* echoing in his ears. Her scent filled his head and oddly enough, his shoulder started to settle down. Not that the pain went away completely. There wasn't a woman alive who could distract him *that* much.

But at least he managed a few hours of peace. No crying shoulder. No bulls to ride. No contracts to sign. And most of all, no truth nagging at him, because, as determined as Pete was to sign the damned contracts, he didn't really want to. He'd gone from being a nobody to a somebody by being wild and free and reckless. The leader of the notorious Lost Boys—*the* most talented group of riders on the circuit so-called because they hailed from the same small town of Lost Gun, Texas. Pete was their poster child. He lived for the thrill of the moment, and Western America was all about the future. About supplementing his income when the fun ended and he was no longer raking in the cash. While the contract wouldn't actually keep him from climbing onto a bull, it would still send a powerful message that Pete

Gunner was getting older, wiser and it would certainly end his career as PBR's favorite badass.

But none of that mattered as he sat there, listening to Wendy Darlington snore softly just a few feet away. Instead, he fixated on the sound and let his troubles slip away along with the pain. And then for the first time in a long time, he actually fell into a deep sleep.

4

SHE HAD *THE* WORST CRICK in her neck.

The pain edged its way past sleep until Wendy finally opened her eyes. She blinked once, twice and reality quickly crashed down around her.

Pete Gunner sat on the opposite side of the table, a pile of pancakes drizzled with sweet-smelling syrup in front of him. He wore nothing but a pair of jeans and a smile. His shoulders were broad, his chest solid and tanned and muscular. Golden swirls of hair spread from nipple to nipple before whirling into a funnel that dipped below the table's edge. A bucking bull tattoo blazed across one thick biceps. Muscles rippled and flexed as he scooped a bite, and her mouth went dry.

"Good morning." His deep, sexy voice snapped her back to reality and the all-important fact that there was sunlight streaming through the windows.

Oh, no.

She bolted upright and winced at the pain at the base of her skull. "This can't be happening." Her gaze swiveled to the window and she blinked against the stream of brightness. "I slept all night? The *entire* night?"

"A whopping six hours." He shoveled in a mouthful of pancakes and chewed.

"It's six-thirty? In the morning?"

"I thought we already established that," he said after he'd swallowed.

"Have we been driving all night?"

"With the exception of a thirty-minute stop, yes."

"Where exactly are we?"

"Texas."

She gave him a *duh* look. "Exactly where in Texas?" She glanced sideways and caught a glimpse of Welcome to Pinto Creek on a road sign that flew by. "Pinto Creek?"

"For about the next five minutes, then we'll be in Lost Gun. And then home."

"How far is that from Dallas?"

"Three hundred and twenty-six miles." He motioned to a mile marker that rushed by. "And counting."

"This can't be happening." Panic bolted through her and she pushed to her feet. As if there were any place to go. "Why didn't you wake me up?"

He shrugged. "People get grouchy when you wake them up. For all I know you could be some kind of early morning crazy who threatens to murder the first person that taps them on the shoulder. I like breathing too much, especially when I've got a mean bull coming up in Boulder next week."

The mention of bulls snagged her back to the all-important fact that the papers still sat untouched on the table between them.

"You still haven't signed."

"I never sign anything before breakfast. I can't concentrate on an empty stomach." He held up a forkful. "Pancake?"

Her stomach grumbled at the sight, reminding her that she hadn't had anything since the chocolate bar she'd wolfed down at the rodeo arena.

Woman doth not live by candy bars alone.

Lisa's voice echoed in her head. Best friend and serial-dater Lisa was always encouraging Wendy to go out with someone—anyone—and have some fun.

But at twenty-eight, Wendy wanted more from a man. Sure, she liked doing the nasty as much as the next red-blooded female, but she wanted a real relationship to go with it. And while she didn't have her heart set on marriage just yet, she at least wanted a man who was open to the concept.

That's what she told herself, but her gaze snagged on Pete's mouth anyway. A dab of syrup sat at the corner and she had the overwhelming urge to lean across the table and lick it off.

Crazy.

She shook away the notion and fixed her gaze on the papers. "I *really* need to get these back to corporate for a counter-signature." The bus swayed to the left as it made a sharp turn and she clutched the edge of the chair. "The sooner that happens—" she fought to regain her composure "—the sooner you get your check." She dangled the one advantage she had over him. Money. It was more than they'd ever paid to any spokesperson in the history of Western America and it was a heck of a lot more than the payout on any old bull.

A gleam lit his eyes before taking a nosedive into the deep blue depths. "I never talk money before breakfast, sugar." He downed a large gulp of milk that sloshed slightly in the glass as they rumbled down what was now a dirt road.

She watched his Adam's apple bob as he took another bite and a strange tingling started in the pit of her stomach.

It was the bus, she told herself. They were pitching and rocking. Enough to hollow out anyone's stomach.

Except his. He seemed immune.

She knew the feeling. She'd lived her life on the road at one time and nothing had bothered her. Not traffic. Or turbulence. Or a rough stretch of road.

Then.

But now things were different. *She* was different. Even if she had slept like a baby for the past six hours.

"So why don't you like pancakes?" he asked as they hit a pothole and she clutched at the chair's edge.

"Who said I don't like pancakes?"

"I offered to share and you turned me down."

"It's not that I don't like them. I just don't happen to want one right now." Liar. She wanted one desperately. A bite of his pancake. A bite of him.

Whoa. Back the horse up.

Where had that thought come from? She didn't want anything from Pete Gunner except his signature, which obviously wasn't happening until he finished the mountain on his plate.

She drew a deep, shaky breath and tried to tamp down on the anxiety rolling through her. Gripping the chair, she slid around and sank down again before she broke an ankle.

Unearthing her cell phone, she spent the next few minutes doing her best to ignore Pete and his pancakes while she checked her voice messages.

Ten from Lisa wanting to know how things were going and when she would be back home. One from her dad telling her he would have a six-hour layover in Houston next week on his way to a Cubs' alumnae dinner. One from Fred telling her not to come back without the papers in hand.

Ugh.

"You missed yoga this morning," Lisa said when she picked up on the second ring. Lisa had been her first friend at Western. The first friendship she'd ever had that had lasted longer than six months. "Are you still in Dallas?"

"Not quite." She watched Pete take a great big bite. Syrup dribbled down his chin and before she could stop herself, she licked her lips. He grinned and she gave herself a great big mental slap. "I, um, think this is going to take a little longer than I anticipated."

"But you'll be home by tomorrow, right? My parents are coming over to meet Mike and I want to finish painting my living room first. I need you to help."

"You guys just started dating two weeks ago. Isn't it a little early to spring him on your folks?"

"What can I say? When it's right, it's right."

"Wasn't it right with Wayne about three months ago? And Marty before that? And Kevin last year?"

"Mike is way better than all of them." *At the moment.* Wendy was willing to bet Lisa would find something wrong with him when things started to get a little too serious. Just as she'd done with Wayne. And Marty. And Kevin. "Listen, can I borrow your red dress? He's taking me out for a special dinner tonight and I don't have time to comb the mall for a new outfit."

"Only if you pick up Tom and Jerry for me. I doubt I'll be home until late tonight."

"On second thought, maybe I'll swing by the mall—"

"They're not that bad."

"They ate my cell-phone case."

"They thought it was a Twinkie and I promise it

won't happen again. You know I've been taking them to obedience classes. Please," she added when Wendy hesitated. "I'll throw in the open-toe shoes."

"I still think I'm getting the raw end of the deal, but okay."

"You're the best." Wendy killed the connection and glanced up to find Pete looking at her.

He arched an eyebrow. "Tom and Jerry?"

"A golden retriever and a Chihuahua." She meant to stop there, but he kept looking at her as if he expected more and the words slipped out on their own. "My mom passed away in a car accident when I was just a few months old. My dad traveled a lot, so I spent way too much time staring at the inside of a hotel room. He bought me videos to help pass the time. I had every cartoon collection out there, but the *Tom and Jerry* ones were my favorites." A smile tugged at her lips. "My dogs are always roughhousing and fighting, and so the names seemed to fit. What about you?" Not that she cared, but it was better to talk than sit quietly and lust after him. "Any pets?"

"Just one."

"And?" she prompted when he seemed hesitant to continue.

"A miniature Yorkie named Tinkerbell."

"It figures."

"What's that supposed to mean?"

"You're the cowboy who refuses to grow up. I should have known you'd have a sidekick named Tinkerbell. But a Yorkie? What kind of a self-respecting badass buys a dog that can double as a powder puff?"

He shrugged. "I didn't pick her. She picked me. Somehow she ended up scavenging around this old rodeo arena just outside of town. She managed to jump up into the back of my pickup and follow me home one night. She's been with me ever since."

She had a quick visual of him cuddling a tiny, yapping Yorkie and her chest hitched.

The realization made her back go ramrod-straight. So what if he had a dog? That was no reason to go all soft and gooey inside. He was still a major thorn in her side.

Still wild and crazy Pete Gunner.

"Living out of a suitcase doesn't exactly lend itself to pet ownership," she pointed out, suddenly desperate to kill the vision of him cuddling a ball of fluff. "That's why I never had one when I was growing up. How do you do it?"

"My ranch foreman looks after her when I'm away."

"Lucky you."

"There's no luck involved, sugar. It's all hard work."

"I'm sure signing autographs is hell on the knuckles."

If she didn't know better, she would have sworn that she'd struck a nerve. He frowned. "I do a lot more than sign autographs."

"I forgot. You also dodge responsibility."

Silence stretched for a tense nanosecond as he eyed her. "Apparently I'm not too good at it because here you are." His frown turned into a full-blown grin. "Then again, I might be a damned sight better than I give myself credit for—" he motioned to the passing scenery, reminding her of the six and a half hours she'd just slept away "—because *here* you are."

"You're a jerk."

"Keep up the sweet talk—" he winked "—and I'll surely be scribbling my signature before breakfast is over." Challenge gleamed hot and bright in his gaze, daring her to say something else, wanting her to. As if he liked the verbal sparring.

Crazy.

Men like Pete usually had a big head to go with their bad-boy reputation. They were used to having their egos stroked, not deflated, but Pete seemed different. Maybe she was imagining things. Even more, she was making her situation that much harder. The point was to coax him into signing, not piss him off.

She clamped her mouth shut and shifted her attention to the window while he went back to his breakfast. Pastureland stretched endlessly as they rolled along for the next ten minutes before the landscape gave way to haystacks and a sprawling one-story house with a gigantic wraparound porch.

"Home sweet home," Pete announced before shoveling in his last bite. He pushed from the table and slid the plate into a nearby sink. The bus took a left and started down the long lane leading up to the house. Pete reached into the stainless-steel refrigerator and pulled out a pitcher of what looked like a lime-green slushie. "Margarita chaser," he offered when she arched an inquisitive eyebrow.

It figured.

If the rumors were even close to the truth, he would probably follow that up with a six-pack and then pull a few Hooters' girls out of the closet.

She shook her head and he turned his attention back to the pitcher. Without bothering with a glass, he downed half of the container before finally coming up for air.

"Don't you think you should slow down a little?" she asked as they started to slow. "I need you sober to sign this."

"Don't worry, sugar. I can do just about anything under the influence. I'm sure I'll be able to scribble my

John Hancock." He set the remainder of the pitcher on a nearby countertop as they rolled to a complete stop. He grabbed the T-shirt draped across the back of his chair and pulled it on just as the bus door powered open.

"If you could just do this really fast for me," she said, blocking his path toward the door. "I'll be out of here in a flash—"

"I knew you'd make it!" The excited voice came from the doorway.

Wendy turned and her elbow slammed into the pitcher, knocking it onto its side. Margarita oozed over the countertop and dripped onto the floor.

She snatched up a dishrag and wiped at the mess just as a tall, lanky young man bounded onto the bus. He had the same killer-blue eyes as his older brother and the same whiskey-blond hair, which brushed the collar of his red-and-blue plaid Western shirt.

"A promise is a promise." Pete grabbed Wade Gunner in a quick bear hug while Wendy wiped at the spilled margarita and frantically scooped as much as she could back into the pitcher.

"You're just in time, too," the young man told Pete. His eyes flashed with excitement. "It's happening."

"Right now?"

The boy's head bobbed. "She's about to pop any friggin' second."

"Hot damn!" Pete exploded. "That's my girl." He headed for the door on the heels of his younger brother and panic bolted through Wendy.

She dumped the last of the iced drink into the sink before her gaze dropped to the pale green stain on the front of her shirt. Great. Now she was going to reek of tequila.

Except she didn't.

She caught a whiff of the almost-empty pitcher and smelled only fresh-squeezed lime juice and the sharp, pungent scent of vitamins.

Wait a second—

Her speculation stalled as she realized the counter was clear. Pete had bolted, and taken her contract with him.

"You forgot the pen—" She started after him, but his long strides had him yards ahead of her by the time she lunged off the bus. He was a man on a mission.

That's my girl?

His words echoed in her head and her throat tightened. In all their meetings on the topic of Pete Gunner, her boss had never mentioned anything about a significant other. Just a long list of temporary flings while he was on the road, including a week with a recent Country Music Association award winner and a few weekends here and there with a Victoria's Secret pinup.

She thought of the margarita that wasn't really a margarita and the Yorkie named Tinkerbell. Maybe Pete Gunner wasn't half the badass he pretended to be.

Just as the notion struck, a grizzled voice echoed in her ears. "The name's Eli," said the old man who stepped up next to her. "Why don't you follow me up to the house and I'll help you get settled into a room?"

Settled? She shook her head. "No, thanks, Eli. I'll be leaving shortly. I just need to get that contract back from Pete and then I'm on the next cab out of here."

He belted out a laugh. "First off, darlin', there ain't no cabs around these parts. And second, if you're thinking to disturb Pete, you'd better think again. When he's with DeeDee, he don't like to be bothered."

"Which one is she? The singer? The lingerie model?"

"Hell's bells, gal, DeeDee ain't no singer and she

sure-as-hell ain't no dad-blasted underpants model."
The man laughed again, his belly shaking with the effort this time. "She's his horse."

"EASY, GIRL." PETE SOOTHED the animal and gathered
the slippery bundle in his arms for one more tug. The
animal gave a loud snort and the foal slipped out in a
tangle of arms and legs.

He handed over the animal to the vet who'd driven
out for the occasion and turned his attention back to
the black cutting horse stretched out in front of him.

DeeDee whinnied and lifted her head before settling
it back down on a pile of straw.

"I know, girl." Pete stroked her smooth flank. "You're
plum tuckered out."

He knew the feeling. Six hours of sleep and he could
still feel the exhaustion tugging at his muscles. Which
made no sense whatsoever because Pete Gunner was the
friggin' Energizer bunny. He'd pulled all-nighters time
and time again. Hell, he'd be pulling one tonight once
the celebration for Wade's birthday got under way. They
had fireworks. Barbecue. Music. It was going to be one
hell of a party and he was damned excited about it.

His heart sure wasn't pumping overtime because
of Wendy.

Sure, he liked the way she smelled and the way she
wiggled her nose when she slept and he even liked her
smart mouth. Despite the fact that she wanted something from him, she wasn't the least bit anxious to im-
press him. A fact that stirred his curiosity.

But not his lust.

At least that's what he tried to tell himself for the
next few moments as he soothed his tired horse.

Seriously, she was a pain in the ass. Sneaking onto

his bus. Cornering him in the shower. Bullying him while he ate his pancakes. Following him all the way home. Just who did she think she was? All she had to do was send him the damned papers and he'd sign them. He *would* sign them.

Not this set in particular, of course. His gaze went to the discarded paperwork lying next to DeeDee and the slimy substances blurring the words. He'd meant to be more careful, but then DeeDee had crowned and he'd forgotten everything except the foal. Western would just have to send out another one.

Then he would sign. Probably.

And then it was on to another PBR title, even if half the world expected him to give it up once he had the Western money in his pocket. That's what battered veterans did. They gave in to their aches and pains, signed endorsements and stepped aside to give the newbies their shot. Not Pete. Bull riding was his thing. The one thing that had kept him going in the early days when having his own ranch had been just a pipe dream and he'd been living in a trailer in Lost Gun with his five-year-old brother and his alcoholic mother. She'd rammed her truck into a telephone pole on the way to the liquor store when he was barely sixteen. He and Wade had been on their own ever since.

But he'd made it. He'd started riding in local rodeos for whatever purse had been offered, and he'd kept riding all the way clear to his first championship. And he'd kept going after that, not just because of the money, but because when he was on the back of that bull, he felt as though he was in control of his life, a master of his own destiny, and that meant everything to a kid who'd watched his mother slip away night after night, powerless to stop her downward spiral. She'd taken him and his brother down with her, until Pete had managed to climb atop that first bull.

"Everybody's comin' tonight," Wade said, effectively drawing his attention and distracting him from his thoughts. "Even Ginny."

Ginny Hooker was the daughter of J. R. Hooker, the local sheriff and the meanest son of a bitch Pete had ever had the misfortune to run into. J.R. was strict, holier-than-thou and he hated the Gunners and the Lost Boys.

A feeling that had been born way back when Pete was thirteen and he'd "borrowed" old man Riddle's horse and ridden it down Main Street, right up to the fountain in the town square. The animal had taken a crap just inches from the water and J.R. had hated him for that ever since. Even worse, Pete had taken in a handful of lowlifes—at least that's what J.R. called them—and given them a second chance.

The Lost Boys had been just that at one time—lost, lonely, destitute. Boys without a home or a family or a purpose. Pete knew what is was like to be alone and struggling, and so he'd given them a place to stay and a chance to make something of themselves. They were now the hottest riders on the circuit and the family he'd never had.

J.R. didn't see it that way. He despised the Lost Boys, and Pete even more for being their leader.

Rightly so. The whole town knew that Pete went out of his way to yank the sheriff's chain. Partly because J.R. was a pompous ass who thought he was better than everyone, but mostly because it was just so much fun.

Why, he would have ridden DeeDee down Main Street tonight if she'd been in any kind of shape.

Pete held tight to the thought, ignored the crying in his shoulder that told him he wasn't going anywhere except into another hot shower and arched an eyebrow at his brother. "Does J.R. know his pride and joy is coming out to our place tonight?"

Wade frowned and handed Pete a blanket for DeeDee. "Probably not, but it doesn't matter. Ginny's almost eighteen. She can do what she wants. And James will be here."

James was J.R.'s oldest son, Ginny's older brother and a once-upon-a-time bull rider. Pete had trained with him way back when and they'd actually forged a friendship based on mutual respect. A fact which made J.R. hate Pete that much more.

"Besides," Wade went on, "the sheriff might not like me now, but that'll change. Once Ginny and I get married and have kids—"

"Wait a second," Pete cut in. "You're not telling me—"

"No, no. We're not getting married *now,* and we sure as shootin' ain't having a kid. But after she graduates college and I win the PBR finals, it'll be time. We won't let anyone stop us then."

"After *you* go to college and *then* win the PBR finals," Pete added, relief washing through him.

"Ain't that what I said?"

"No, you said Ginny was going to college and you were going to the PBR finals."

Wade shrugged. "What difference does it make?"

"It makes all the difference in the world. I already told you, you're not climbing onto a bull in a professional arena unless you've got a degree under your belt. That was our agreement. I'll teach you everything I know while you go to school, but you're not hitting the circuit until you graduate."

"About that…" Wade started and Pete shook his head.

"There's no 'about that.' You're going to college, Wade. We already talked about this."

"I'm much better with bulls than I am with calculus."

"All the more reason to stick it out. Just because something's tough doesn't mean you quit." Their mother had quit on them by drowning herself in a bottle, an example Pete never intended to follow. "We don't quit." He eyed his brother. "You and me, we *never* quit." Not back when he'd been dirt-poor with a six-year-old depending on him, and not now that he had his own spread and a great career.

When his little brother didn't look half as certain as Pete felt, he added, "I bet Hooker would be even more inclined to come around if his daughter was settling down with a college-educated bull rider." Not that J.R. would ever come around as long as Wade's last name was Gunner, but Pete didn't want to say that. Not when Wade looked so hopeful.

"You think so?" Wade asked.

"It's worth a shot. That is, if you *really* like this girl."

"I don't like her, Pete. I love her." Wade said the words with such conviction that Pete almost believed him. Except that Wade was young, his hormones raging, and it was too damned easy at his age to mistake lust for love.

What's more, Pete didn't necessarily believe in love. Not the give-it-all-up, do-anything-and-everything-to-hold-on-to-it kind that people wrote about in books and bad country songs.

Lust?

Now *that* he believed in.

He pictured a certain stubborn marketing executive and his groin tightened. Okay, so maybe he *was* lusting after her. How could he help himself? They had chemistry. Fierce. Immediate. Inexplicable.

While he couldn't begin to understand the pull, it was still there. Burning him up from the inside out and making him want to forget everyone and everything and take her to bed right here and now.

If only Wendy was a here-and-now kind of hookup. She'd watched her father live in the fast lane, however, and so she'd put the brakes on in her own life. She was settled now, and he wasn't. Settling down meant slowing down in Pete's book, and that was the last thing he ever intended to do.

Even if his aching shoulder had other ideas.

No, as much as he wanted to, he wasn't sleeping with Wendy Darlington.

"We'll talk about all this later," he announced, eager to get out of his own head and forget the damned heat licking at his nerve endings. He finished covering DeeDee with the blanket and pushed to his feet. "Right now we need to get cleaned up." He grinned and winked at his younger brother. "It's time to party."

5

THIS WAS CRAZY.

Wendy glanced at her watch for the umpteenth time as she paced the front porch of the massive ranch house. She'd been waiting for Pete Gunner for hours and he still hadn't come out of the monstrous red barn sitting just beyond the corral.

And when he eventually did make it out, she had the gut feeling he wasn't coming out with the signed contract in hand.

Which was why she'd come prepared with an extra copy.

She'd almost marched number two down there after the first hour had ticked by, but Eli had stopped her. He'd insisted she join him for breakfast in the big kitchen. Then he'd taken her on a tour of the ranch. *Then* he'd forced her to play dominoes. And throughout it all, he'd told her story after story of how he used to ride the rodeo circuit and how he could still rope with the best of them. And how she really ought to consider signing a more seasoned man to represent Western American.

They were parked on the porch now, watching a massive truck unload dozens of picnic tables just beyond the corral. The barbecue pits had started hours earlier and the musky scent of mesquite filled the air. A stage had been erected and the band had already started setting up. In the far distance, a John Deere front loader stacked wood into what she guessed was going to be a massive bonfire.

"Modesty aside, y'all put too much emphasis on selling stuff to these wet-behind-the-ears young 'uns." Eli's voice drew her around. "Why, they ain't got a nickel in their pocket to spend on all that expensive hoorah that you all sell. Now a man like me is a different story. I got a nice chunk in the bank, an even nicer chunk under my mattress. I can appreciate the finer things. There's a load of folks my age who buy from Western. I'm sure the female customers would break open the piggy bank if they saw a fella like me all decked out on some big poster hanging over the cash register." He sipped the glass of tea in his hand. "What do you think?"

"I think I've been waiting here long enough." She paced the length of the porch yet again.

"Slow down there, girlie. This ain't the big city. We like to take our time out here. Kick back. Relax. You ought to try it. It might help those two pinch lines between your eyebrows."

She came to an abrupt stop and touched her forehead. "I don't have pinch lines. Do I?"

"All's I'm sayin' is a woman your age has to be careful about stuff like that." He shrugged. "Say, did I tell you about the time I roped this nasty sumbitch horse called Smoochey over in New Mexico?"

"Yes and can we please stop talking?" Eli grunted and she started pacing again. Two steps this way. Two steps that way. Three steps this way. Three steps that way. Her temples pounded and anxiety rushed up and down her spine. The seconds crept by.

"So where do you live?" she finally asked after several silent moments that made her even more nervous than his constant bragging.

"I thought you wanted to stop talking?"

"I changed my mind. So where do you live?"

"Nearby."

"A neighboring ranch?"

He nodded toward the front door of the massive house. "You're looking at it."

"You live here? With Pete?"

He nodded. "And Wade. And Tinkerbell, here," he scratched the tiny Yorkie behind her small ears. She licked frantically at his hands and he fed her a tiny bit of sugar cookie. "And the Lost Boys, too."

"The Lost Boys?" Her mind rifled through the various articles she'd read about Pete Gunner. The Lost Boys, so-called because they all hailed from the same small town of Lost Gun, were his protégés. They weren't champion status yet, but they were gaining serious momentum on the rodeo circuit. She'd read that Cole Chisholm, a twenty-year-old bronc rider and one of the infamous Lost Boys, had caused an uproar in Phoenix when he'd unseated the reigning champion. Rumor had it he was good. They all were.

Rumor also had it that they were the wildest bunch of riders on the circuit. Now she knew why. They had Pete Gunner, the king, as a daily example.

The hum of an electric guitar sizzled through the air as the band started its sound check and she glanced yet again at the big red barn.

"Just 'cause you keep starin' don't mean he's going to come out of there."

"He has to come out sooner or later."

"I wouldn't lay any bets on that."

"What are you saying? That he's never coming out?"

"I'm saying, sugar dumpling, that he already came out. About a half hour ago."

"What?" Her gaze swiveled to the barn, then back to Eli. "No way. I've been standing here for the past hour. I would have seen him."

"Not if you're too busy yapping."

"I wasn't yapping. That was you."

"Oh, yeah. Let me rephrase that—" He fed Tinkerbell another bit of cookie. "You probably didn't notice on account of you were too busy being captivated by all my yapping." He seemed to stop and listen. "So much so that Pete made it all the way into the shower and you didn't notice a thing."

"You're saying he's in the house?" She pointed to the massive structure. "This house? In the shower?" She didn't wait for a reply. She snatched up the second set of contracts and marched inside.

Upstairs, she followed the sound of spraying water down the massive hallway, into the far wing of the house. Sure enough, she soon found herself in a man's bedroom, a familiar pair of boots kicked into the far corner.

Pete was in the shower, all right. Meanwhile, she'd been standing around outside, waiting for him.

The man had no manners. Worse, he had no sense of responsibility.

That's what her head told her. He was a wild child who had his priorities twisted.

Her heart, however, said something altogether different. Like, maybe, for whatever reason, Pete Gunner was dodging her on purpose because he really didn't want to sign.

She remembered the way he'd eyed the contracts, the push-pull of emotion in that split second before his it's-all-good mask had slid back into place.

Not that it mattered. She hadn't come all this way to go back empty-handed. If he didn't want to sign he should never have accepted in the first place. He'd done just that and she meant to see that he followed through.

The sound of running water pulled her closer until she stood inches away from the bathroom door.

She thought about knocking. She really did. But judging by what had been happening, she couldn't help but think that he might crawl out the window if he got any advance notice that she was on to him.

Taking a deep, steadying breath, she pushed open the door and walked inside. The bathroom was huge with wall-to-wall tile and an open shower in the far corner. Steam filled the bathroom and coated it with a mist that made her feel sticky and hot.

She opened her mouth, but the words lodged in her throat as her gaze riveted on the very naked backside of Pete Gunner.

Water sluiced over his shoulders, running in rivers down his corded back, his toned buttocks. Her brain registered the absence of tan lines and immediately she had a vision of him completely naked, riding a single rope out over a cool lake on a hot summer's day.

He turned to the side and gave her a magnificent view of his profile.

Rubbing a bar of soap between his hands, he spread the lather over his chest, his six-pack abs and down over the sprinkle of hair that led to his crotch. His penis was thick and strong, surrounded by a swirl of silky hair.

Her mouth went dry and her heart stalled. She should say something. He was naked, for heaven's sake! Even more, she wasn't the kind of woman who stood around lusting after naked men.

Then again, she didn't get the opportunity very often, and as much as she tried to remember this wasn't what she'd come for, she just couldn't seem to tear her gaze away.

He was all hard muscle and raw strength and she could feel her body responding in ways that had nothing to do with her eagerness for him to sign the papers and everything to do with raw desire. Her heart pounded and her hands trembled.

"Enjoying the view?"

At the sexy drawl, her attention snapped back to his face and her gaze locked with his. A lazy grin tugged at the corner of his mouth.

"I…" She swallowed, desperate to find her suddenly shy voice. *Get a grip, Darlington.* "You still need to sign these…" The request didn't come out nearly the way she'd rehearsed over the past several hours. There was no commanding note in her voice. No air of authority. Not even a plea of desperation. Instead, the words were choked and soft and almost an afterthought.

"You *are* enjoying the view." He grinned. "Don't worry. So am I."

"But I've got my clothes on."

"Doesn't matter." His gaze fixed on her chest and she glanced down to see that all the steam had made her white silk blouse practically transparent. "You've got beautiful nipples, sugar."

A rush of heat went through her and she glanced down to see one traitorous bud peaking through the lace of her bra, perfectly outlined by the see-through silk.

She stiffened, determined not to turn tail and run despite the fact that he was staring at her as if he wanted to take a great big bite.

And even more, she was feeling as though she wanted him to do just that.

She stiffened and tried to gather her control. "I need the contracts signed."

"I'm afraid we had a little accident."

"I thought as much." She held up the second set. "Just sign already and let's get this over with." She swallowed. "Please."

"And what if I don't?"

"You don't get your money."

"I doubt concern for my financial well-being brought you three hundred miles out of your way." His gaze darkened. "And straight into a naked man's bathroom. What really happens if I don't sign?"

She wasn't going to tell him. It wasn't his business. At the same time, the words sprang to her lips and she couldn't help herself. "I lose my job."

He killed the water and reached for a towel. Before she could take a much-needed breath, he was standing right in front of her. "You should stop worrying so much. It ages you."

The teasing light in his eyes made her forget all about the papers and the pink slip waiting for her should she fail. "You're the second person who's told me that today." He arched an eyebrow and she added, "Eli said the same thing."

"Great minds," he murmured. "It's just a job."

"It's my job and I happen to like it."

"Why?"

"Because I've been there for nine years and I want to be there another nine years. I like Houston. I like being in one place. I like having friends." Now why had she said that?

Because it was true and there was just something about his compelling gaze that drew the words from her.

"Houston's nice," he murmured, "but I like Dallas better. And Vegas. And Nashville."

"You really like being on the go that much?"

He didn't answer. Instead, something flitted across his expression and she got the instant feeling that he wasn't half as content with his lifestyle as he wanted everyone to think.

"I like being a rodeo cowboy," he finally said.

"An irresponsible rodeo cowboy." She held up the extra copy she'd brought. "Or so you want everyone to think, which is why you don't want to sign these papers."

His brows drew together into a tight frown. "What are you talking about?"

"You let me believe you were drinking margaritas this morning." She wasn't sure why she called him out except that she was tired of playing games. "It was a vitamin slushie."

"Like hell."

"You also didn't want to tell me that you had a Yorkie named Tinkerbell. You're this big, bad, supposedly irresponsible guy who doesn't care about anyone or anything, yet you've got a house full of guys living here and you keep Eli gainfully employed when he has to be the most annoying man I've ever met. You're also getting your ass kicked up on that bull, but you don't want to admit it—or any of the above—to anyone because you're afraid it's going to kill your image. That's why you don't want to sign. Because signing would be the responsible thing to do."

"You're full of shit."

"Prove me wrong, then," she countered. "Right here and now."

Just like that, his gaze darkened as if she'd stripped off her clothes and pressed herself up against his wet body.

"What do I get if I do?"

"Fame and fortune."

"I've already got both."

"You'll get more."

"What if I want something else instead?"

"As in?"

The seconds ticked by as he stared down at her. He looked almost hesitant. A glimmer lit his eyes as if he wanted to say something. But then the light faded into a dark, smoldering blue as his attention settled on her mouth. "A kiss might just do the trick."

"You want me to kiss you and then you'll sign?"

"That, or I can just kiss *you*." And then he did just that.

He dipped his head. His mouth caught hers in a plundering kiss that took her breath away. His deep, musky scent filled her nostrils. His body heat drew her closer. Her nipples tightened and an ache started between her legs. And she couldn't help herself. She leaned into him, molding herself to his hard frame despite the fact that he was soaking wet. The alarm bells in her head faded into the pounding of her own heart, and suddenly there were just the two of them and the kiss.

A kiss that quickly morphed into something softer and more persuasive when she wrapped her arms around his neck and angled her head to give him better access. His arms slid around her waist, drawing her even closer. His tongue swept her bottom lip and dipped inside, stroking and coaxing and drawing a raw moan from deep in her throat.

It was a kiss like no other, and just when she was really getting into it, he drew back.

He stared down at her, his breathing hard, his blue eyes dark and unreadable, as if he couldn't quite believe what had just happened. The look faded quickly, however, into a teasing light.

He grinned and reached around to pat her on the ass cheek.

The sudden motion jolted her from the daze of the passionate kiss and she came to her senses. "Are you going to sign the papers now?" she managed to say with stiff lips.

"Can't." He shook his head, staring down at the contracts which had landed in a puddle of water at his feet. "I'm afraid they're ruined." And then he waltzed past her and headed for the adjoining bedroom. "On the bright side, we've got a hell of a party ahead of us so the night isn't a complete bust."

The slam of a door punctuated his words and she was left standing in the steamy bathroom, staring at the soggy papers on the floor.

A party?

Did he really think a party was even in the realm of possibility with her future hanging in the balance?

That would have been her father's solution for just such a problem. He never worried too much about anything. Instead, he would have hit the nearest bar to show the world that no matter what the breaks, he was still baseball's favorite rowdy boy.

No way was she waltzing outside to watch Pete and his cretin friends feed the rumor mill that already surrounded them. She was a professional and it was high time she started acting like one. He'd toyed with her enough and no wonder. Every time he looked at her, she forgot all about her job and morphed into another one of the countless buckle bunnies who melted at the first touch.

Distance. That's what she needed.

She needed to get on her cell, have another contract sent out ASAP, and then call a cab. She would check herself into the nearest motel and wait him out. He had to sign eventually.

And if he didn't?

She forced aside the thought. He would. However wild and reckless, he hadn't made it to the top of the PBR heap by being stupid. The deal was a good move, particularly since she knew beyond a doubt that Pete wasn't as young and wild as he wanted everyone to think.

As young and wild as *he* wanted to think.

She'd seen the flash in his eyes when she'd called him out. She'd hit a nerve, even if he didn't want to admit it.

He would. He was taking a beating and it was just a matter of time before it caught up to him.

In the meantime, she was going to establish some boundaries and show Pete Gunner that at least one of them could behave responsibly. And she wasn't—repeat *was not*—going to think about his kiss and the fact that she'd liked it a lot more than she should have.

She'd seen too many women fall for her father and get their hearts broken as a result.

She wouldn't be like those women.

Even if Pete Gunner had given her the most exciting kiss of her life.

6

SHE WAS STUCK HERE.

Wendy came to that realization the moment she got off the phone with the town's one and only cab company.

Red's Cabs. Only in reality there was no *s* in "Cabs"— Red just went with the plural form for advertising purposes, or so he'd told her. He had one car and he was currently busy picking up a special supply of imported dog food from the nearest airstrip—over an hour away—for the mayor's wife. By the time Red got home, had his supper and drank his milk, it would be time for *Dancing with the Stars*.

Bottom line? She wasn't going anywhere until tomorrow morning.

So much for establishing some boundaries and a safe working distance with Mr. Wild and Irresponsible.

Even more upsetting, Lisa had already left with Mike and wasn't picking up her phone. Wendy had left a message about having new contracts sent out asap but she knew nothing could happen until Monday morning.

She stared at her reflection in the mirror, her gaze drawn to the plain black skirt and white buttoned-up blouse. She'd worn almost the exact same outfit to the company Christmas party last year. It was like all the other outfits in her closet—functional, conservative, low-key.

All except for the red dress Lisa had given her for her birthday. The dress screamed *Do me,* which was why Wendy hadn't actually worn it yet.

Rather, she'd stuck with the classics because they were reliable. Even more, they projected that *she* was reliable.

A far cry from the women who'd drifted in and out of her dad's life. His longest relationship had been with a groupie who'd followed him to training camp one year. He'd kept her around approximately three weeks before ditching her via voice mail. Wendy could still see the woman standing on the doorstep in a hot-pink dress cut down to there and up to here, hoping to pour her heart out to him and change his no-commitment policy.

A wasted effort.

Mitch Darlington had sworn off relationships when he'd lost his wife of four years in a car accident and had been stuck with a toddler. He hadn't wanted anything permanent and so he'd sought out women who looked more temporary. Party girls who'd put it all out there with their skimpy clothes and trashy talk.

Wendy wanted more, and so she'd made sure to dress the part. To attract the right man.

Like Jim the accountant.

She tried to conjure an image of the mild-mannered accountant, but for some reason, she couldn't. Instead, she kept seeing Pete's smiling face, the flash of guilt in his eyes when she'd called him out. The glimmer of denial.

Ugh.

The sound of the band kicking up carried through the window, effectively distracting her from her thoughts. She walked over to take a quick peek.

There were already people everywhere. In the distance, pickup trucks, Jeeps and SUVs roared down the dirt road, congregating in the field just to the left. It seemed as if the entire town had turned out for Wade Gunner's eighteenth birthday.

Her gaze hooked on a trio of identical women standing near the dance floor. Long, lustrous dark brown hair, lots of makeup, big chests and tiny waists. They wore cut-off blue-jean short shorts and pink cowboy boots. The tiny white tee stretched across their ample breasts read The Lost Boys...Cowboy Up!

Buckle bunnies.

Even worse, they were half-dressed buckle bunnies who oozed sex appeal.

If only she'd stashed her skimpy red dress in her bag before she'd left Houston.

Excuse me? She wasn't here vying for Pete Gunner's attention, even if deep down he wasn't as wild and reckless as he wanted everyone to think. He was still walking the walk and talking the talk, and so he was off-limits. More important, she was here as a representative of Western America. A professional. Despite the kiss in the bathroom.

A fluke. That's all it had been. Her deprived hormones. His well-calculated ploy to keep from signing the papers.

And it wasn't happening again.

Gathering her determination, she headed downstairs to the kitchen. A quick snack and she would tackle the work in her briefcase. She'd just hit the bottom step when she heard a commotion behind her at the top of the stairs.

She stepped to the side just as three figures came barreling down.

"Give it back." Wade Gunner wrestled with two men, one blond and one a brunet, desperately reaching for the hat that the dark-haired one held beyond arm's reach. "It's my new Resistol."

"Finders keepers," said the brunet.

"That's right," said the blond. "Ain't you ever heard? Possession is nine-tenths of the law."

"You're full of horse shit," Wade said. "Now give."

"What do you think, Billy?" The brunet eyeballed the blond holding Wade's arms. "Should I give it back?"

"I don't know, Jesse. Seems to me we ought to make him beg a little more."

"Have a heart, guys. It's his birthday," Wendy reminded the two men who held a frustrated Wade captive.

Pete's younger brother looked as if his head was about to blow off and her heart went out to him. He didn't stand a chance against the two muscular males who finally let him loose and started tossing the hat back and forth between them.

"And who are you?" The dark-haired man chanced a glance at her in between throws.

"Pete brought her here," Wade said, and just like that, the hat landed in his hands.

The two men wiped their hands on their jeans and thrust them toward her.

"The name's Billy Chisholm," the blond told her, giving her a full grin.

"Jesse Chisholm," offered the brunet.

She knew they were related even before she heard the

names. While Jesse appeared dark and dangerous and Billy looked more like the boy next door, they still had the same eyes. Deep violet with gold flecks that seemed to twinkle as they stared at her. They wore starched Wranglers, pearl-snapped shirts and spit-polished cowboy boots.

"Are you members of the Lost Boys?"

They exchanged glances. "Darlin', we *are* the Lost Boys."

"That's not true," Wade blurted, plumping up his now caved in hat. "There's four more of 'em."

"Yeah, but two are team ropers, one's a barrel racer and the other's a bronc rider. Everybody knows they don't count," Billy said, giving her a wink. "I ride bulls."

"Yeah," Jesse added. "So do I and I'm better at it."

Billy glared at Jesse. "Says who?"

"The judges' panel over in New Mexico. I kicked your butt last week."

"You've got a short memory, 'cause I distinctly remember being the one to kick your butt." Billy shook his blond head and turned to Wendy. "Listen." He gave her a smile that had undoubtedly charmed many a girl out of her panties. "I placed higher overall in rankings last year, so if you're looking for someone for your next campaign, I'd be perfect." He gave her a wide smile that said he wouldn't mind getting his picture taken for a living.

There was no denying that he had the looks. And the personality. But they needed a well-known face, and while everyone who followed the pro circuit had heard about the Lost Boys as a collective group, she'd be willing to bet that very few had ever heard of Billy Chisholm.

Not yet, that is.

"I'm afraid we've already got a spokesperson for the upcoming season." Or they would just as soon as Pete Gunner got his act together and put his name on the dotted line. "But I'll keep you in mind."

"Me, too," Jesse said. "'Cause my name is gonna be bigger. That's a promise, little lady."

"Bigger than what?" The question came from another cowboy who headed down the stairs. He was a few inches shorter, but just as well-built as the other two. Hot on his tail was his spitting image except that his medium-blond hair was a little shorter.

"These are the twins," Wade told her. "Jimmy and Jake Barber. They're team ropers."

"More members of the Lost Boys?"

"You know it," Jimmy Barber told her. He pointed behind him to two more men descending the stairs. "There's the last of the group." He pointed to another brunet with a red gingham cowboy shirt and dimples that would make any woman swoon. "That's Buck Davis, barrel racer and general badass, and that scary looking thing behind him is Cole Chisholm, resident bronc rider. He's Jesse and Billy's brother." He motioned to the tallest of the bunch who had sun-kissed brown hair and the same violet eyes as the first two men. "Cole don't like getting all fancied up." Which explained why the man wore faded jeans, a T-shirt with a rip in the sleeve and a look that said *I'll tear you a new one later if you don't shut the hell up.*

"I like getting dressed up just fine, but this is a barbecue. No reason to put on my church clothes."

"The Barbie triplets are here," Billy reminded him.

Cole's eyes widened a split second before his brow pulled into a frown. "You're messing with me."

"Honest to God," Billy added. "Saw 'em pull up myself just a few minutes ago."

Cole's gaze made the rounds before settling on Wendy. She nodded. "If they're the three identical brunettes rocking pink cowboy boots, then I saw them, too."

"Dammit to hell." Cole turned and bounded back up the stairs, taking two at a time.

"Slow down," Billy called after him. "It don't make no nevermind what you look like anyhow. Those gals don't give a lick about you. They're here to see yours truly."

Cole shouted down a colorful example of where Billy could go and how fast he could get there before Wade chimed in. "It's my birthday, which means they're all here to see me."

"Who we talking about?" Pete asked as he rounded the corner.

"The Barbie triplets," Jesse offered.

Pete grinned and Wendy's heart practically stopped. *What the hell?*

Here she was, smack-dab in the middle of cowboy central, and not one of the Wrangler-clad hotties, not even the three sexy Chisholm brothers, made her feel even a fraction of what Pete stirred up in her.

Her heart revved, her stomach flipped and a tingle swept the length of her spine. Her lips trembled in memory of the heated kiss they'd shared upstairs and her traitorous hormones kicked in. Just like that, she found herself thinking again about her skimpy red dress.

"You boys better get a move on. The place is filling up fast." He turned his attention to Wade. "I saw a certain yellow Mustang pulling into the south pasture."

"Uh-oh," Jesse Chisholm drawled, flicking a lock

of Wade's hair. "No wonder he spent an hour getting all prettied up."

"Did not." Wade slapped at Jesse's hand, smoothing his do back into place. His shirt was tucked in and his boots gleamed. Wendy couldn't help the smile that crept across her face. "I needed a shower, is all." He shrugged and glared at the group surrounding him. "You all try birthin' a foal."

"Leave him alone," Pete said to the smiling bunch. "And get on outside. We've got guests."

The cowboys ambled past, tipping their hats to Wendy as they went. Jesse paused just a few seconds longer and gave her a wink. "You'd better save a dance for me, Miss Wendy."

She didn't have the heart to tell him she wasn't going to the party, so she just smiled and nodded.

"If you know what's good for you, you'll steer clear of Jesse."

Pete's deep voice slid into her ears and she turned to find his gaze hooked on her, a dark look on his face, as if he wasn't too pleased at the thought of her dancing with someone else.

As if.

Pete Gunner wasn't any more possessive than the man on the moon. He floated from female to female and she'd do well to remember that.

A traitorous thrill vibrated up her spine anyway. "And what's so wrong with Jesse?"

"It's common knowledge he keeps time with anything in a skirt. It's all about quantity for him."

"Isn't that what it's all about for you? No, wait, that's just an act."

"Like hell it is—" he started, but then the sound of Eli calling his name cut him off. His grin was quick and easy, and her stomach hollowed out. "The more the merrier, sugar," he drawled. "So are you going to add yourself to the list and give me another kiss?" The question was straightforward and to the point. Exactly what she expected from rodeo's resident bad boy.

Her reaction, however, wasn't at all what she anticipated. Not after her mental tirade about distance and professionalism. Her throat went dry and her stomach hollowed out and her lips tingled. Desire rushed through her, drenching her from head to toe.

"While I don't think you're half as bad as you want everyone to think, I still seriously doubt a kiss is all you want," she finally managed to say, eager to remind herself that he was the worst kind of player.

He chuckled, the sound a warm rumble up and down her spine. "No, but it's a damned good start."

She gathered her courage. "What happened upstairs was a mistake."

"The only mistake is the one you're about to make by being stubborn and wasting a perfectly good opportunity to spend the evening with me."

"You really are full of yourself, aren't you?"

"It's called being practical. You're stuck here." He shrugged as if he didn't care one way or another, but his eyes gleamed with an intensity that told her he was more invested than he wanted her to think. "You might as well make the most of it."

"By kissing you?"

"That, and a few other things." His gaze darkened. "It's the damnedest predicament, but I can't seem to stop thinking about you."

"I bet you say that to all the girls."

"As a matter of fact, I do. I just don't usually mean it." His gaze locked with hers. "There's just something about you…" He stared at her as if he didn't any more understand the sizzle between them than she did. "For whatever reason, things heat up pretty quickly between us, and I can't help but wonder just how hot it can get. It's all I can think about, as a matter of fact. You. Me. Sex." The last word skimmed across her nerve endings and firebombed in the pit of her stomach.

No. That's what she should have said. Right before she turned on her heel and walked away from him and his ridiculous offer. Pete Gunner was far, far away from what she wanted in her life.

But maybe, just maybe, he was exactly what she needed at the moment.

The thought struck and instead of pushing it away, she let it simmer for the next few moments. She was three hundred miles from the real world, stuck on a ranch for the next forty-eight hours with a man so irresistible that it made her teeth ache. If she gave in to the lust raging deep down inside, she could sate her deprived hormones, stop acting like a nymphomaniac and remember her objective. If not, it was sure to be the longest night of her life.

Doubt pushed and pulled at her and she thought of her father. Of all of the women who'd drifted in and out of his life. She'd vowed never to be one of those women.

She wasn't.

While she might be contemplating one night with Pete Gunner, no way was she going to actually fall for him and get her heart broken. She was too smart for that. She knew a man like Jim was what waited in her future.

But right now… Right now it wasn't about her heart. It was about satisfying the lust gripping her body and blowing off some steam.

He knew it, and so did she, and suddenly there seemed nothing wrong with spending the next few hours together.

"Okay." The words slipped out of her mouth before she could stop them. "Let's do it."

He wasn't the least bit surprised. Obviously. He was Pete Gunner. Irresistible to all women. He didn't know the meaning of the word *rejection*. At the same time, she didn't miss the flash of relief, as if he needed her just as much as she needed him.

Hardly.

She had no illusions about his attraction to her. He'd been with oodles of females. Drop-dead gorgeous ones that were no doubt much better in bed than she could ever be. The only reason he wanted her was because she didn't want him. Once she gave in, the heat would soon fizzle. She would become just another notch on his belt. Another conquest to feed his womanizing reputation.

But damned if she felt like one.

Staring up into his brilliant blue eyes, she felt like the most beautiful woman in the world.

The woman.

At least for the moment, and right now that was enough. She slipped her hand into his.

Surprisingly, however, he didn't lead her upstairs. Instead, he threaded his fingers through hers and turned toward the front door.

Wait a second.

While she'd just committed to have sex with him, she wasn't going to spend the next few hours watching him feed his reputation as the state's biggest party boy.

She dug in her heels. "Shouldn't we head upstairs and get to it?"

He winked. "I knew there was a bad girl lurking in there somewhere."

"It's called being practical," she said, throwing his words back at him. "I want you. You want me. No sense putting it off." The sooner she spent the lust eating away at her, the sooner she could forget all about Pete and climb back onto the straight and narrow.

"There are five hundred people outside, sugar. I have to put in an appearance." He grinned that infamous grin that made her want to strip naked and beg him to kiss every inch of her body. "Unless you're afraid you won't be able to keep from jumping my bones in front of everyone. If that's the case, we can stop off at the broom closet on our way out and save you the public display."

He was playing on her precious control, and damned if it wasn't working. "I hate to break it to your overinflated ego, but I think I can contain myself long enough for you to play the dutiful host."

Or so she hoped.

Especially when his eyes twinkled and he murmured, "We'll see about that, darlin'. We'll just see about that."

7

SHE'D ACCEPTED his offer.

He was definitely surprised at that, but not half as much as he was that he'd made the offer in the first place.

He'd been ready to run at the first sight of her tonight. She spelled trouble with her know-it-all attitude. She had his number and she made no bones about dangling that information in front of him, which made her dangerous with a capital *D*. He didn't want a woman to dig down deep and psychoanalyze him. He wanted to keep being the infamous Pete Gunner.

He would.

But then he'd seen Jesse looking at her like she was the last piece of pecan pie at a Sunday social, and he'd felt a surge of jealousy. An emotion a man like Pete wasn't the least bit familiar with. It had turned him every which way but loose and suddenly the thought of not sleeping with her scared him a hell of a lot more than the fact that she was all wrong for him.

She felt right.

Too right.

Which was why he'd brought her outside instead of

straight to his room. With a crowd of people around reminding him who he was, maybe he could actually get his head on straight before they did the deed.

That's what he told himself as he introduced her to James Hooker and spent a few minutes talking about the new arena the man had planned.

He made the rounds then, stopping to welcome everyone and share a few jokes and ask if they'd had plenty to eat. He found out that Sue Ann Jenkins was expecting twins, and the money he'd donated to the library was helping to buy books for a new wing, and the mayor had just announced he was going to run for a sixth consecutive term.

The beer flowed and the barbecue sizzled on the grill. An upbeat Kenny Chesney song lured people onto the dance floor. And Wendy Darlington drank it all in like a third-grader staring through the window of the local candy store.

He noted her cover-everything-up blouse and her plain black skirt. A complete contrast to the half-clad women belly-rubbing their way across the dance floor. His chest hitched and he had the sudden vision of her as a young kid. Shy. Naive. Holed up in a hotel room when she should have been running across a playground with other kids. He knew what she'd felt. He'd stood on the sidelines at Harding Elementary School day after day, watching the other boys play football or chase. He'd wanted so much to join in, but he'd been Vanessa Gunner's son. A bastard. No good. Or so everyone had thought. He'd lived his childhood on the fringes, never really fitting into whatever foster family he'd been dumped into.

Which was why he'd made it his business to be the center of attention as an adult. He was always right in the thick of things. Setting the pace. Dictating the game. Holding all the cards. The one in control.

He had the feeling that by walking the straight and narrow, Wendy was doing exactly the same thing. She was exercising control of her own life, steering it in the opposite direction of her father's, and missing out on life in the process.

Excitement.

While she wouldn't admit it, he could see it in her eyes, feel it in the tremble of her hands.

"Let's kick up some sawdust and show these folks how it's done."

Excitement glimmered a split second before the doubt set in. "I don't think that's such a good idea."

"Come on, sugar. It'll be fun."

"I'm sure it would be. If I knew how."

He squeezed her fingers just enough to let her know that she wasn't alone. "You'll do fine," he murmured, his voice soft, reassuring.

A few seconds ticked by before she finally nodded.

He led her onto the dance floor and pulled her into his arms. The two-step had faded into a soft, twangy song about green tractors.

Her arms slid around his neck. Her perky little breasts with the cranberry-colored nipples pressed against his chest Her pelvis cradled his, moving against him with a soft, subtle sway that sent a bolt of electricity straight from his hard-on to his brain.

The jolt scrambled his sanity, and instead of pushing her away and running for safety because she was the last type of woman he needed in his life, he pulled her even closer and closed his eyes.

Her hair tickled the underside of his jaw. Her strawberries-and-cream scent filled his head. Her luscious curves pressed against his hard body. Her warmth seeped inside and made his blood rush faster.

"What do I do?" her soft voice pushed past the lust beating at his brain.

"Just hold on tight and follow my lead."

Her arms tightened and heat spiraled through him.

His hand slid an inch lower, easing from the small of her back to the swell of her sweet little ass molded by her snug skirt. His other hand slid up her back and he tugged her ponytail loose. Her hair spilled down over his hand as he cupped the back of her neck. His fingers pressed into her flesh and his thumb drew lazy circles against the tender spot just below her ear. She sighed— a soft, breathy sound that whispered through his head and sent a jolt to his cock.

The chemistry flowing between them was more powerful than anything he'd ever felt before. Add to that the fact that he'd been so damned busy lately he hadn't been rolling around the sheets nearly as often. Hell, it had been more than six months since he'd been with a woman.

All the more reason to steer her away from the dance floor, up the stairs to his bedroom and get to it. He'd fulfilled his duties as host. He could slip away right now and no one would be the wiser.

"How am I doing?"

Her soft voice slid into his ears and he noted the way her body followed his as if she'd been doing it all her life.

As if they were made for each other.

The thought struck and he stiffened.

"What's wrong?" She stared up at him, her green eyes glittering beneath the swirl of lanterns. Her forehead wrinkled and he had the sudden urge to reach up and smooth the lines away with his fingertip. "Pete?" Surprise turned to concern. "Are you okay?"

"Um, yeah. I just need to check on the ribs."

"What?"

Yeah, *what?*

"The caterer was running short on ribs and I need to make sure they were able to get some extra sent out from town." And then he turned and got the hell out of Dodge before he did something he would surely regret.

Like fall hard and fast for Wendy Darlington.

As hard as his little brother had fallen for Ginny Hooker.

His gaze strayed to the young man and the pretty little brunette in his arms. Neither danced very well, but it didn't seem to matter as they fumbled their way across the makeshift dance floor. They only had eyes for each other and Pete felt a pang of envy.

A certifiable feeling if he'd ever had one. Wade was just infatuated and Pete knew better than anyone how fast that eased. Once a man kissed a woman, touched her, loved her, the feeling faded. It always had in the past and Pete had no doubt that would be the case for Wade. Even if his little brother did think he was head over heels at the moment.

Infatuation. That's all it was. It sure as hell wasn't love. Not for Wade and certainly not for Pete himself.

No matter how well Wendy Darlington kissed or how her body molded against his when they danced or how she seemed to see right through the charade that had become his life.

Bad boy Pete Gunner didn't fall in *love,* for Christ's sake. No sirree. He didn't get hooked and have crazy thoughts, like wanting to see a couple of kids playing out in the pasture instead of a mess of monster trucks.

Kids? Hell, he'd never really thought about kids or settling down or *anything*.

He didn't think. He acted.

Until now.

The thought struck and sucker punched him right
in the gut. Before he could double over, however, he
heard the big, booming voice and a wave of *holy shit*
rolled through him.

"I told you these boys were responsible."

He glanced toward the fringe of the dance floor and
sure enough, J. R. Hooker stood there flanked by two
deputies from the sheriff's department. Hooker was
tall and meaty, testimony to the fact that he'd played
offensive lineman at Texas A & M back in the day. He
wore a large Stetson, a starched Western shirt and stiff
Wranglers. A badge covered his pocket. A massive dia-
mond ring glittered on his hand as he waved it toward a
few of the Lost Boys who sat at one of the picnic tables.

"They did it." He pointed at Jesse and the others and
the deputies stepped forward. "They're the ones who
helped that boy kidnap my Ginny."

The music faded as one officer grabbed Jesse and
the other went for his brother Billy, and all attention
focused on the ruckus.

"We didn't kidnap your girl," Jesse protested.

"Damn straight we didn't." Billy glanced at Pete's
kid brother. "And neither did Wade."

"That boy is now officially eighteen," J.R. growled,
motioning toward Wade. "I want him arrested and
thrown in with the adults."

"Nobody's getting arrested," Pete said as he walked
straight into the heart of the commotion. "You know
Wade didn't kidnap Ginny," he told J.R.

"She said she was going to study at Lizabeth Slater's

house. She never made it, which tells me she was accosted against her will."

Pete's gaze went to Ginny, who now stood behind her father, looking scared and intimidated and guilty as all get out. His heart went out to her because he'd heard what a loud-mouthed bastard J.R. could be and he'd seen it firsthand more times than he cared to admit. She cast hopeful glances at her brother James who stood nearby. But James wouldn't step in and Pete didn't want him to.

This was between him and J.R.

The sheriff hated him and rightly so. Every time he looked at Pete, he saw his past mistakes. Instead of making up for them, J.R. wanted to erase them entirely and that meant running Pete and the Lost Boys out of town once and for all.

"My brother didn't do anything wrong," Pete said again before turning to the deputy holding Jesse. "Lyle, you know Wade wouldn't do such a thing, and Jesse and Billy sure wouldn't help him."

Lyle shook his head. "It's not up to me to make that decision. If the girl says she was kidnapped, then Sheriff Hooker has every right to press charges. Then it's up for a judge to decide."

Pete turned his attention to Ginny, but she seemed to close up. She stared at her feet, refusing to say a word. He didn't miss the tremble in her hands. "Don't do this," he said, turning his attention to J.R. "It's just a misunderstanding. Drop it and we'll forget all about it."

"I'm not dropping anything. I want these boys arrested. Each and every one of them."

Lyle finished popping the cuffs on Jesse and Billy, and then turned his attention to Wade. He was just about to snap on the cuffs when Ginny's voice rang out. "Stop!

He didn't kidnap me. I came here because I wanted to, Daddy. I wanted to."

J.R. didn't look half as surprised at the news as he did mad that she'd opened her mouth in the first place. "You most certainly did not. No daughter of mine would associate with this kind of scum."

"He's not scum. He's wonderful," Ginny cried out.

"He's trash. Always has been, always will be."

Pete's mouth drew into a tight line. "If you don't get him out of here," he told Lyle, "I'm going to press some charges of my own for trespassing and harassment."

"I'd like to see you try," J.R. said.

"Now," Pete added. The deputy obviously didn't miss the edge in Pete's voice, and he acted accordingly. He released Jesse and Billy and Wade, and turned to J.R.

"We ought to be leaving now, Sheriff. Looks like this misunderstanding has been cleared up."

"This ain't the end of it," Hooker added. "I ain't putting up with this. You tell your brother to leave my little girl alone if he knows what's good for him."

The kicker was, Ginny *was* good for Wade. When he'd met her, he'd barely been passing any of his classes. She made him want to be a better person. To try harder. To think instead of rushing headfirst into the rest of his life.

Even more, she saw him for the man he was.

Like Wendy saw Pete.

She was the only one who'd ever seen beneath the surface. The only one to call him out.

His gaze went to where she stood on the sidelines, obviously shaken by what had just happened. Her gaze met his and he felt the crazy hitch in his chest. A reaction that had nothing to do with lust and everything to do with the fact that he actually liked her. The way she smelled. The way she smiled. The dogged determination. The unmistakable compassion. The understanding.

Yeah, right. They'd just met.

Yet in the short time that they'd been together, she'd seen more of him than any woman ever had before, and he'd seen her. The fear when she spoke about her past. The determination not to follow in her father's footsteps. Even more, he understood about wanting to change the past, to run from it, to stay one step ahead. He'd been doing it his entire life.

Like her, he still was.

But maybe, just maybe he wouldn't mind slowing down if he had Wendy to slow down with.

Crazy.

That's what he tried to tell himself as he spent the next few hours playing the dutiful host and avoiding Wendy as much as possible. He threw down a few shots with his neighbor and twirled the prettiest girls around the dance floor, and did his damnedest to ignore the woman who watched from the sidelines.

He did his damnedest to forget her, but he couldn't. She'd gotten under his skin, into his head, into his heart.

No. What he felt was purely physical. He *knew* that. He'd gotten hooked on women before; one roll in the sack and bam! They'd been off his radar.

Wendy would be no different. That's what he told himself as the night wound down and everyone started to leave.

And there was only one way to prove it.

WENDY GRABBED THE BOTTLE of honey and squirted a dollop of golden liquid on top of one warm biscuit. She sat at one of the picnic tables and watched the band pack up the last of the instruments. Most of the lanterns had gone out and the guests had left. The few who remained had climbed into their trucks and hightailed it out to the bonfire that burned in the far distance. The lead singer for the band climbed into the cab of his truck, the engine grumbled and Wendy found herself alone watching the lights flicker in the far distance.

It had been hours since the chaos with the sheriff's department and everybody seemed to have forgotten the drama.

Everyone except for Pete. She'd seen the strain in his face, the fear behind his perpetual grin. He'd been afraid for his brother and her heart tightened at the realization. Pete wasn't half the wild child he'd pretended. If he had been, he wouldn't have threatened to have J. R. Hooker arrested for trespassing, he would have thrown a punch. And another. And another.

He'd talked his way out instead. Albeit forcefully, but still… Pete wasn't nearly the irresponsible, immature, hot-to-trot cowboy everyone thought he was. He had his act together. He just didn't want to admit it.

Rightly so. He'd made a fortune playing PBR's wild child. He'd be crazy to stop now.

Wendy, however, liked seeing the grown-up version. She liked it way too much.

She took another bite of biscuit and tried to ignore the truth blaring inside her head. Pete Gunner had changed his mind about their deal.

She didn't blame him. She'd seen all those women tonight. Buckle bunnies with their long legs. And fake boobs. And bottled tans. The place had brimmed with them and it didn't take a rocket scientist to figure out that Pete had finally come to his senses. Why would he lust after a woman like her when he could have his pick?

He wouldn't. Maybe that bull hadn't just battered

his shoulder. Maybe he'd suffered a concussion and he hadn't been thinking clearly. He was back to his old self now. As bold and as bad as ever.

Thankfully.

That's what she told herself. Sex would only complicate their working relationship. At the same time, she couldn't deny the frustration brimming inside her and the all-important truth that she'd wanted him to come running back for another dance, another kiss and more. Much more.

She popped a bite into her mouth, the gooey sweetness oozing over her fingers. Sliding a fingertip into her mouth, she licked the honey and went for another bite just as she heard the footsteps behind her.

She turned to find Pete standing there. He'd shed his Western shirt and wore just a white T-shirt that outlined his broad chest and clung to his muscular biceps. Faded jeans cupped his crotch and molded to his thighs. His whiskey-blond hair curled down around his neck. A five-o'-clock shadow covered his jaw.

She found herself suddenly desperate to feel the stubble chafing against her cheek, and lower, down the slope of her neck, the rise of her breasts, her nipples, the tender insides of her thighs....

She got to her feet, ready to make a quick retreat inside the house before her hormones got the best of her. He'd already made it painfully clear that he'd changed his mind tonight. No reason to make a fool of herself and beg.

She drew a deep breath and tried for a calm tone. "I figured you'd be at the bonfire by now." Trucks roared in the distance and music blared.

"A deal's a deal, sugar." And then he closed the distance between them and reached for her.

8

HE BACKED HER TOWARD the table, a dark, desperate gleam in his gaze. "This is all about sex, right?"

"Definitely."

"We're not dating." He said the words as if his life depended on them.

She shook her head. "I would *never* date a man like you."

"That's what I was hoping you'd say." He gripped her by the waist and sat her atop the picnic table.

"What are you doing?" she asked when he reached for the buttons on her blouse and started sliding them free.

"What I should have done the minute you said yes." He pushed the shirt over her shoulders and down her arms. His fingers went to the clasp of her bra and she spilled free. The cool night air whispered over her bare skin and her breasts throbbed.

"Here?"

"Right here." He stared deep into her eyes. "Right now." His gaze dropped to her bare breasts. "You have the most incredible nipples I've ever seen." There was

no missing the admiration in his gaze, the appreciation, the *want*.

At that moment, she stopped worrying that someone
might happen upon them or that she wasn't the type of
girl to strip down buck-naked on a picnic table. She
didn't care. She simply wanted him. His hands everywhere. His mouth on her. *Now*.

"I wanted to peel off your clothes and touch your
nipples so bad earlier tonight, and I wanted to taste
them. I *really* wanted to taste them."

Before she could drag in a breath, he dipped his head
and drew one sensitive peak into his mouth.

He sucked her so hard and so thoroughly that it was
all she could do to keep from sagging against him. Wet-
ness flooded the sensitive flesh between her legs and
drenched her panties. He drew on her harder, his jaw
creating a powerful tugging that she felt clear to her
core.

An echoing throb started in her belly, more intense
with every rasp of his tongue, every nibble of his teeth,
every pull of his sinful lips.

Heat flowered through her, pulsing along her nerve
endings, heating her body until she felt as if she would
explode.

He didn't touch her with his hands, just his mouth,
working at her until she moaned long and low and deep
in her throat. Her nipple was red and swollen and throbbing when he finally released her to lick a path to the
other breast. The tip of his tongue rasped her ultra-
sensitive flesh. Goose bumps chased up and down her
arms. The hair on the back of her neck prickled.

"Please," she murmured, and he gladly obliged, seiz-
ing the other nipple and delivering the same delicious
torture. Pull and nibble. Pull and nibble. Pull and...

Ahhh…

She grew wetter and hotter, her body throbbing with each movement of his mouth as he worked her, pushing her closer to the edge, to a mind-blowing orgasm.

She opened her mouth to tell him to stop. It was bad enough that she wasn't nearly as experienced as he was. She wasn't spouting like Old Faithful and proving it beyond a doubt. But then his mouth was on hers, swallowing her words, his hot fingers rolling and plucking her damp nipple, and all thought flew south to the wet heat saturating her panties and the steady, frenzied throbbing between her legs.

He pulled her flush against him, his hands trailing down her bare back, stirring every nerve ending along the way. Fingers played at her waistband before grasping the edge of her skirt and pushing it up higher until his palms cupped her bare buttocks. He urged her forward, pushing her legs open wider and pulling her tight against him until her pelvis cradled the massive erection straining beneath his zipper.

The feel of him sent a burst of longing through her and suddenly she couldn't get close enough. She grasped his shoulders, clutching at his T-shirt as she wrapped one leg around his thigh to fit herself more snugly against him. She kissed him with all of the passion that had built over the past few hours.

Her tongue danced with his and she sucked, drawing him deeper, wanting more yet not getting enough. When he tore his lips from hers, a whisper slipped past her swollen lips.

"Don't stop," she gasped. "Please. I don't know what I'll do if you stop." She was pathetic, she knew. Not a one of the hot blondes that had attended his party would have stooped to such a level.

They didn't have to.

She waited for his infamous grin, that teasing light in his eyes. Instead, his gaze darkened to a stormy blue.

"I'm not going to stop." Conviction rang in his voice and her chest tightened.

His fingers went to the button on her skirt. The waistband eased and he peeled the material down her legs. His fingers snagged on her panties and urged them down, as well. Until she sat completely naked.

He urged her lips apart in another deep, mind-blowing kiss as he lifted her. He wrapped her legs around his waist, his denim-covered erection flush against the sensitive folds between her legs.

The sudden contact drew a gasp from her lips. She grasped his shoulders and shimmied against him. The friction of the rough material against her clitoris worked her into a frenzy, until she couldn't take any more. She threw her head back as a deep, pleasure-filled moan vibrated up her throat. Delicious tremors rocked her body.

"Holy hell, you're beautiful."

She heard his deep, raw voice through the thunder of her own heart and his words sent a rush of joy through her. She didn't stop to tell herself she was imagining things or that they were all wrong for each other or that she shouldn't be falling for him when she'd promised herself not to. Instead she concentrated on the sincerity in his voice and let it feed the satisfaction gripping her body.

She was so lost in the throes of her orgasm that she didn't even notice that he'd carried her inside the house, up the stairs and into his bedroom until she felt the soft mattress at her back.

She glanced up in time to see him peel off his shirt and unfasten his jeans. He shoved the denim and his white briefs down in one smooth motion. His erection sprang forward, huge and greedy. A white drop of pearly liquid beaded on the ripe purple head and slid down the side. She couldn't help herself.

She reached out and caught the drop on her fingertip. She touched the moisture to her lips and tasted the salty sweetness before dipping her head and taking a lick.

He groaned at the sight of her lush lips brushing the length of his cock. He gripped her silky hair, guiding her as she pleasured him for a few heart-pounding moments. But where a soft warm mouth would have been enough in the past, it wasn't enough now because this wasn't just a nameless, faceless woman who'd popped up in his bed. This was Wendy and he wanted to give as good as he was getting. Better, in fact. Not because he had an image to protect, but because he wanted to see her come apart in his arms. He wanted to feel it. To savor it.

He gripped her shoulders and urged her to stop. Leaning over, he reached into his pocket and pulled out a condom. He smoothed it over his throbbing length in one deft motion, and then he leaned over her, pushing her into the mattress as he urged her legs apart and settled himself between her trembling thighs.

He kissed her then, licking her lips and sucking at her tongue, tasting the ripe flavor of sex and loving it because it was his.

She was his.

The thought struck, echoing in his head as he drove into her with one powerful thrust.

She was tight, grasping the full length of him with enough force to make him groan.

He lay still for a moment. "You feel so damned good. So tight and wet and hot."

"You feel good, too. So big and hot and hard." She couldn't believe she'd said such words, but she couldn't help herself. With his voice so deep and stirring in her ears, Wendy felt her control melt away. She stopped worrying about the past or the future and simply lived in the moment.

She slid her arms around his neck and arched into him, determined to get closer and savor every moment: the weight of his body between her legs, the tickle of his hair against her most sensitive spot, the weight of his testicles resting between her thighs.

He spread her legs even farther apart and pushed deeper for a split second before withdrawing. The movement was slow and tantalizing, and a wave of pleasure swamped her. He stopped just shy of pulling out, the head of his penis pulsing inside her.

Before she could draw her next breath, he thrust deep again, sending a burst of heat through her and making her nerves sizzle.

He pumped faster with each thrust, driving her toward an orgasm while he worked toward his own. She clutched at him, raking her nails down the length of his back, grasping his buttocks, pulling him deeper as she lifted her pelvis to meet each of his movements. She couldn't feel him deep enough or hard enough or fast enough….

Her climax built, bucking her up and jerking her back down like the wildest rodeo bull. Up and down, higher and higher, faster and faster, until she finally reached the last second. The buzzer sounded and she went flying off into the air. Her heart pounded. Her blood rushed. Her body sang with exhilaration.

She cried out and felt him stiffen. She opened her eyes just in time to see him poised above her. His entire body tensed as he threw his head back, his teeth clenched. Every muscle tightened and bulged as he reached the pinnacle of his own wild ride. He exploded in a loud groan that echoed in her ears.

He rolled onto his back, pulling her on top of him without breaking their contact. His heart pounded against her own and his breaths came sharp and ragged.

Wendy rested her cheek in the curve of his neck and fought for a calming breath. She needed to gather her wits, to think.

Impossible with him so close.

She could only feel. The tickle of his hair against her chafed nipples, the hot slickness of his thigh on the inside of her own, the length of his penis nestled in her sensitive folds. He was still semi-hard. The large, smooth head twitched and pulsed with each of his deep, shuddering breaths.

Gathering her courage, she propped her head up on her elbow and stared at him. "There's nothing wrong with slowing down," she finally said, her voice quiet. "If you're tired, take a break. Quit. Cowboys do it all the time."

"I don't need a break and I sure as hell don't quit." Pete didn't mean to snap, but leave it to Wendy to ruin a perfectly good mood by calling him out on something.

His mother had been a quitter. She'd given up on herself and left her sons to raise themselves.

He never quit. Not when he'd been so poor that all they'd had to eat was bologna sandwiches. He'd kept going, struggling, fighting.

He wasn't quitting now.

Even if he wanted to.

He frowned. "Has anyone ever told you that you talk too much?"

"Never."

"Well, they were just being nice because you do. You talk way too much." And then he tucked her up against him and closed his eyes. And for the first time in a helluva long time, Pete Gunner fell right to sleep.

9

"I'M GOING TO OVERNIGHT three sets of contracts so you're covered for any future mishaps first thing tomorrow morning. They should be there bright and early Tuesday," Lisa told Wendy on Sunday morning.

"Thanks, Lisa."

"No problem. I still can't believe they got messed up again."

"Me, neither. What did you tell Fred about the delay?"

"Exactly what you told me. Gunner wanted to sit down with his lawyer, who wasn't available until Tuesday morning to go over the contract line by line as a formality. By Tuesday afternoon, you'll have his signature on the dotted line and we'll have Pete in the studio bright and early a week from today for the first commercial shoot." Her voice grew quiet. "Are you sure you can pull this off?"

"Are you kidding? It's practically done." *Not.* They hadn't spent the past night just having sex. They'd also talked—her idea, not his—and she'd come to realize how important his career was to him. Bull riding and all that went with it—the reputation, the attitude, the control—had saved him from his past, just as settling down had saved her. "He'll sign. I'm sure of it." Or so she hoped.

"At least one of us is having some luck with men," Lisa grumbled.

"What happened to Mike?"

"He moved on to greener pastures."

"Don't tell me you dumped him, like all the others, because he wanted to get serious."

"*He* dumped *me* because *I* wanted to get serious. I really think he's the one."

"You're kidding, right?"

"What? A girl can't fall in love?"

But Lisa wasn't just any girl. She was a serial-dater. Playing the field. Avoiding commitment. Just like Wendy's father. "You never fall in love," Wendy said accusingly. "Not in twenty-eight relationships." Because it just wasn't possible for a leopard to change its spots. Her father had had plenty of chances, plenty of women who'd offered him everything, but he'd turned down all of them because he was incapable of settling down.

Or maybe he just hadn't found the right one.

The notion stuck in her head as Lisa went on, "I've actually had thirty-one guys if you count the cashier at the dry cleaners, the bartender down in Cabo and my massage therapist, and, no, I didn't fall in love with any of them. I fell in love with Mike. Don't ask me how or why. I just know I love him and so I told him so. He ran. I should have expected it. It's karma coming back to bite me in the ass."

Wendy was still marveling over Lisa's change of heart when she climbed out of the bed a few minutes later to search for her clothes.

She'd opened her eyes to find the bed completely empty about fifteen minutes ago. No trace of the man who'd loved her within an inch of her life for the past thirty-two hours. If she hadn't had such delicious aches in all the right places, she would have sworn she'd dreamed the past night.

It had been too perfect. Too wonderful. Too right.

And now it was over.

She knew it even before Eli found her on the front porch a half hour later, a coffee cup in her hand.

"Are you ready, Miz Wendy?"

"For what?"

"Pete told me to take you into town."

The words were like a vise sliding around her heart and squeezing tight. Not that her heart was involved in this. Last night had been purely physical. A one-night stand. And while she'd never actually had a one-night stand, she was a grown woman who could handle herself accordingly. They'd had a great time together, end of story. No sense dragging it out or letting her feelings get involved.

But this wasn't about feelings. It was about her future. Her job. "If Pete Gunner thinks he's getting rid of me that easy, he's got another think coming. He promised me a signed contract and I'm not going anywhere until I have it in my hand."

"I wasn't kicking you out. Since you're stuck here," a deep, familiar voice drawled behind her, "I thought you might need some extra clothes. But if you'd rather stick it out in that get-up, be my guest."

She whirled and found the bluest eyes in Texas staring back at her. He wore a blue-and-white striped work shirt, a pair of jeans and dusty boots. The smell of leather clung to him and she barely resisted the urge to press herself up against him and drink in his scent.

He grinned and her heart melted.

Her heart, of all things.

The realization hit her and every muscle in her body went stiff. An image flashed in her mind and she saw the woman in the pink dress standing on her father's doorstep. So hopeful and optimistic and in love.

What the hell was she doing?

Falling for Pete Gunner. The truth was there. Blaring in her head. Mocking her. She'd gone and done the unthinkable.

He winked and her heart skipped its next beat. "You didn't think I was getting rid of you this soon, now did you, sugar?"

She fought down the warmth rolling through her and gathered her courage. She might be falling, but she hadn't hit the ground. Not yet. Not ever. "Actually, yes. I know how guys like you work."

"Guys like me, huh?"

"Wham bam, thank you, ma'am."

"I don't think I've ever called a woman I'm sleeping with ma'am, but to each his own."

"The contracts will be here first thing Tuesday morning," she blurted, determined to remind him—and herself—of the real reason she was here in the first place.

"That gives us plenty of time, then."

"For what?"

"More of last night."

A thrill raced up her spine and she stiffened. "Two more days isn't exactly plenty of time. The contracts are being overnighted."

His grin widened. "That means Wednesday out in these parts. Maybe even Thursday."

"I'd lay bets on Friday," Eli chimed in. "It's sweeps weeks on daytime TV."

"What does that have to do with the contracts arriving Tuesday morning?"

"See, Red is a big soap-opera addict and so he doesn't always make it out to the airstrip on the outskirts of town in time for the delivery. His wife tried getting him to record the programs every day, but he's not much on technology."

"Threw the damned remote at the wall," Eli added. "Cain't say as I blame him. Those damned things would drive anyone crazy."

"Anyhow," Pete went on, "if Red's not there, the delivery gets locked up and he has to wait until the next day at delivery time for the shed to get unlocked. And if he misses that, well, it starts all over again the next day."

"But Red's a cabdriver."

"And the local postman," Pete told her. "He also calls bingo every Friday night over at the VFW hall."

"Sells Amway, too," Eli offered. "I bought this foot lotion off him last week that can't be beat. 'Specially if you got calluses."

"So you're telling me I'm stuck here until Thursday?"

"Or Friday," Eli added, "depending on if Cheyenne comes out of the coma before she has the baby or after she has the baby."

"Cheyenne?"

"From *The Rich and the Reckless*." When Wendy flashed him a surprised look, he shrugged, "What can I say? It's a helluva show."

PETE STARED AT WENDY as she exited the dressing room of the one and only boutique in Lost Gun and the air caught in his chest.

She wore a blue-jean miniskirt that emphasized her

endless legs and a white tank top that hugged her breasts and outlined her ripe nipples.

"This is all she's got in casual wear." She turned toward the woman who stood nearby. "Are you sure you don't have some sweat pants or jeans?" she asked Delilah Simmons, the shop's owner, who'd been more than happy to open up on her day off when Pete had called her.

"I only stock cowboy couture, little lady. You want something else, you got to wait until tomorrow and head over to the feed store. Or you can drive a couple of hours to Austin and find something there. I'm sure they've got plenty of places open on Sunday." She eyed Wendy's reflection in the mirror. "This is what all the young ladies in town are wearing."

Thankfully.

Pete kept the thought to himself and focused on the uncertainty in Wendy's eyes. The expression made him want to reach out and pull her into his arms and tell her how great she looked.

He would have, except he didn't want to complicate things any further. She'd come downstairs with her fighting gloves on and he meant to keep it that way. It would make things that much easier when they said goodbye.

And he *would* say goodbye. Wendy was a forever kind of girl and Pete Gunner couldn't turn his back on the only life he'd ever known.

No matter how much he suddenly wanted to.

In the meantime, however, he meant to make the most of the time they had left.

She turned in a circle before giving him a questioning gaze. "What do you think?"

"Fine," he managed to say in a calm, cool voice that

didn't betray the urge to back her up against that full-length mirror and show her exactly what he did think—that she was the sexiest, the most beautiful woman he'd ever seen.

"I don't know." She seemed almost disappointed by his reaction as she turned back toward the mirror. As if she'd expected more of a reaction. As if she'd wanted one.

"Maybe something a little longer," she said.

"Are you kidding? It's hot outside. That'll do just fine."

"Maybe I should try a sundress."

"Whatever." He swallowed and tried to calm his pounding heart as the red curtain swished closed and she disappeared back into the dressing cubicle.

He'd sworn to himself just that morning that he wasn't going to act interested and give her even the slightest hope for a future together. That's why he stayed away from good girls. He didn't want a woman with expectations.

Until now.

He gave himself a great big mental ass-kicking and focused on the racks of clothing that filled the boutique.

Hick Chicks carried everything from trendy hip-hugger jeans and rhinestoned tank tops to the latest in sexy lingerie.

He eyeballed a pair of camouflage panties and damned himself. Hell, maybe he should have had Mitch over at the feed store open up. They could have picked up a package of Fruit of the Looms and a pair of Levi's.

But he'd wanted to keep his mind on sex and off the picture she'd made that morning sitting on his front porch, the newspaper open in front of her, a steaming cup of coffee on the table next to her. As if she belonged there.

"What about this?" Wendy's voice killed the image and drew him around.

He turned to see her wearing a pale yellow dress with tiny pink flowers. One spaghetti strap inched over her shoulder and he barely resisted the urge to slide it back into place. The dress hugged her breasts and waist and fell to mid-thigh. She looked so sweet and innocent and—

"I think we need something a little more revealing," he said instead, his voice gruff. "Something that screams sex." His gaze caught and held hers. "That's what this is about, isn't it?"

HE WAS RIGHT. If she was going to keep things purely physical between them, she had to dress for sex rather than an actual date.

That's what Wendy told herself when she headed back into the dressing room and pulled off the sundress. Pulling it right side out, she slipped it back onto the hanger and ignored the *Buy it!* screaming inside her. It really was a pretty dress.

Pretty, she reminded herself, not sexy.

She needed sexy.

She reached for an aqua-blue number that the sales clerk had brought in. It was cut up to here and down to there and Wendy felt cold just looking at it. At the same time, it was the exact sort of thing a woman having a fling with rodeo's hottest bad boy would wear. She was just about to shimmy into it when she heard the rustle of curtains, followed by a deep, husky voice.

"I like it."

Excitement rushed through her for several fast and

furious heartbeats, followed by a spurt of panic because she was wearing nothing but her underwear. Practically naked.

Naked is good, she reminded herself. *Sexy.*

She tamped down her nerves and drew a deep, calming breath.

She could handle this. She could handle him.

The curtains swished closed behind him and he simply stood there. He'd changed out of his work clothes before they'd left the house. He looked so tall, tanned and delicious in a red T-shirt and worn, faded Wranglers, the hems frayed around his scuffed boots. He'd left his hat sitting on the dash of his truck so there was nothing except a thick fringe of golden lashes shadowing the intense blue gaze that swept from her head to her toes and back up again.

Her heart thundered and goose bumps chased up and down her bare arms. She reached for the aqua dress and pulled it to her, using the material to effectively cover her breasts as she worked it off the hanger.

"You're really beautiful." The deep, husky words echoed in her head and thrummed through her body. He stood even closer now, his body warm and enticing in the frigid air-conditioning of the dressing room.

He stepped up to her. The scent of him surrounded her and his hard warmth teased her shoulder blades. When she felt his large, callused fingers at her waist, her hand went limp and the dress slipped away. Her head snapped up and her gaze collided with his.

"I don't think this is the right place."

"Darlin', whenever the mood strikes, it's the right place." His hand slid around her waist and trailed down her abdomen to her panties. His fingers skimmed the white cotton triangle covering her sex. "Are you in the mood?"

"I..." She started to say something, but his intimate touch stalled her frantic thoughts before she could come up with something coherent. Reason escaped her and the only thing she could do was nod.

His fingertips burned through her panties. His strong arms surrounded her. His large palm cupped one buttock. His warm breath ruffled the hair at her temple.

"I can't stop thinking about last night."

"Me, neither," she whispered despite the noise coming from just the other side of the curtain. Delilah was a nosy woman and liable to whip the flimsy door covering aside at any given moment.

It didn't matter.

The only thing that mattered was the man pressing her up against the dressing-room wall, his hands roaming her body, making her sizzle with anticipation.

"I'll stop if you want me to." The words came from far away, pushed past the passion beating at her brain and touched something deep inside her she was fighting so hard to keep bottled up.

Her eyes met with his and she saw the strange emotion flickering in the dark depths. She knew deep in her heart he was just as surprised as she was that he'd said the words. But he meant them.

"No," she murmured.

If she'd had any doubts, they slipped away as fast as her panties in that next instant. "I want this. I want you." And then she slid her arms around his neck and held on for the wildest ride of her life.

10

ODDLY ENOUGH, the next few days were the most exciting of Pete Gunner's life.

He admitted that to himself on Tuesday night as he stretched out in his bed, Wendy curled up next to him.

The sound of her deep, even breaths echoed in his ears and he held her tighter.

Sure, the sex itself was exciting, but it was all the rest that sent him over the edge.

On Monday, he'd given Wendy a tour of the ranch and taken her on a picnic and showed her Gunner Bluff at sunset. On Tuesday, they'd toured the small town and had lunch at the diner. He'd told her about his past, about losing his mother and raising his brother and taking in all the other Lost Boys. He'd listened to her talk about her father and how she'd never spent enough time in any one place to really feel at home and how she'd painted her kitchen cabinets yellow and bought a new doghouse for Tom and Jerry, and how she was going to plant a garden next year. And then he'd brought her home to bed and made slow, sweet love to her for hours on end.

Lame.

That's what he told himself. No mud wrestling or wet

T-shirt contests or guzzling beer and running naked around town square.

Yet his heart pounded at breakneck speed every time Wendy smiled at him. And when she touched him? Christ, his adrenaline went through the roof. Eight seconds didn't hold a candle to the way she made him feel.

Not that it mattered.

Pete wasn't giving up his career for anyone, and that's what he would have to do. He wouldn't ask her to follow him around and live out of a suitcase the way she'd done growing up. And he sure as hell wouldn't want her here without him, settled while he slept alone night after night.

No, it was better that she went back to her life and he went back to his.

He just wished that all-important fact didn't suddenly bother him so freakin' much.

"So THIS IS THE INFAMOUS DeeDee?" Wendy asked on Thursday morning as she stood in the barn and eyed the dark brown cutting horse and her foal.

"The best horse in the world, isn't that right, girl?" Pete stroked the animal's shiny coat while Tinkerbell barked and yapped at DeeDee's feet.

Wendy had walked down to the barn, eager to keep herself busy until Red showed up with the contracts. He'd called and said he was on the way and she knew it was just a matter of time before they faced the inevitable.

It was over.

"She was my first horse," Pete went on. "Eli gave her to me way back when. She lost her mom in a lightning storm when she was just a few days old. The animal went crazy and broke her neck. Eli was on the road back then with the circuit and he didn't have time to care for an orphaned foal. I was sixteen and more than happy to help. I nursed her with a bottle, trained her and rode her in my first rodeo. That was back when I was roping. I did some saddle-bronc riding after that. Then came the bulls."

"A jack-of-all-trades."

"When it comes to cowboying. Otherwise, I'm not much good at anything else."

"You're good on this ranch."

"That's cowboying."

"Do you ever think about what you'll do when it's over?"

"Hell, no." He reached for a brush and put his energy into brushing the glossy animal.

"You're lying."

"And you talk too much."

"So I've been told." She arched an eyebrow. "What about it? Surely you know you can't do it forever. It's already taking its toll."

"A few aches and pains are par for the course."

"A few, but I saw you last night." She reminded him of a very acrobatic stint in the shower. He'd groaned from the pain in his shoulder and her heart had gone out to him. "It was bad."

"Not if you don't think about it. You stay focused on the ride, on the purse, and it's all good."

"You're lying." They both knew it, but it didn't seem to bother him as much as it used to. As if he didn't mind that she saw past his barrier. As if he liked it.

Because she was different.

Because he was falling for her.

If only.

She ditched the thought and busied herself by grabbing another brush and helping him for the next few minutes until he finally called it quits.

"Come on," he told her. "I want to show you something."

She knew she should beg off. Red would arrive any minute and the sooner they cut to the chase with the papers, the better.

At the same time, she desperately wanted a few more minutes with him before reality intruded.

"Okay." She twined her fingers with his and let him lead her from the barn.

"IT'S A RIVER." Wendy stood looking out over the glassy body of water after a very bumpy twenty-minute ride on Pete's four-wheeler. They stood on a small ledge that jutted out over the mirrorlike surface.

"Not the river." Pete pointed to a large oak tree that stood nearby, a sturdy-looking rope tied to one of the branches that jutted out over the water. "The swing. Tied it up there when I first bought the place. I'd just started riding and money was tight, so we found our fun where we could. Whenever I come home, I head out here and take a ride over the water." His eyes twinkled as he stared down at her. "There's nothing like it."

Before she could say anything, he stripped down to nothing, grabbed the rope and went sailing out across the water.

"What are you waiting for?" he asked when he came up sputtering.

She eyed the rope before shifting her attention back to him. She felt his gaze stripping her bare even before her hand went to the waistband of her skirt. "An audience," she finally murmured.

It wasn't the sort of thing she would ever say to anyone, but Pete was different. She could say anything to him. Do anything. Nothing shocked him. Even more, nothing shocked her. She didn't get embarrassed or worry that he might get the wrong impression. Or the right one. It seemed natural.

He seemed natural.

For now.

The thought made her all the more determined to make the most of this moment.

She peeled off her clothes, slowly, deliberately until she finally tossed her undies to the riverbank. She gripped the rope, pulled back and launched herself out over the water.

With a squeal, she let go. The cool liquid sucked her under for several frantic heartbeats before strong hands pulled her up to the surface.

She smiled at Pete through watery eyes. "That was great."

"Not half as great as you." His lips touched hers then and he took her breath away with an endless kiss that left her panting.

Their tongues tangled and she had the sudden thought that nothing could be better than right here, right now.

This.

Not her house with the yellow cabinets. Or the garden she meant to plant next year. Or her job and the great big promotion waiting for her once he signed his name on the dotted line.

And he would sign. She had no doubt about that. Sure, he'd been hesitant, but if there was one thing she'd learned about Pete over the past few days it was that he kept his word. He'd promised to take care of his brother all those years ago and he'd done just that. He'd promised Eli to take care of him when he grew too old to make his living as a rodeo cowboy, and he'd done that. He'd taken in the Lost Boys and he was helping them establish a name for themselves.

He would sign.

Even if she wasn't so sure she wanted him to.

The realization hit her as he carried her onto the riverbank, stretched her out on the soft grass and leaned over her. The sun outlined his massive form and edged his hair in a bright gold. He was tired. She'd seen it in his eyes when he moved his shoulder a certain way. She saw it now as he leaned over her, though she doubted he minded the pain all that much at the moment.

She touched his temple and traced the outline of his jaw. He needed to slow down. Deep inside, he wanted to. He was just afraid to admit it.

She knew the feeling.

She had her own fears. Losing her job. Giving up her home. Turning into her father. Ending up with a man just like him.

But Pete wasn't Mitch Darlington. He cared about people, and while he still lived out of a suitcase and fed his bad-boy image, he wasn't cold and selfish and afraid of commitment.

He was afraid of losing control. Of losing everything he'd worked so hard for and winding up the sad, lonely kid he'd once been.

But things were different now. *They* were different and it was time to lay the past to rest once and for all.

And suddenly Wendy knew exactly what she needed to do.

PETE'S HEART DID a double thump as he walked into the television studio bright and early Monday morning as promised.

Not because he was about to shoot his first commercial and blow his bad-boy image to hell and back by looking like a sellout.

Wendy would be here.

"Hells bells, boy." Eli's voice drew him around to see the old man coming out of the men's room. "What in tarnation are you doing here?"

"Making a commercial." Pete frowned. The last he'd seen of Eli, the man had said he was heading to Vegas to play the slots before they left for New Mexico and the Turner County Rodeo Finals. "What are you doing here?"

"Making a commercial of my own." The minute Eli said the words, Jesse Chisholm walked out of a nearby dressing room, a cowboy hat cocked back on his head, a grin on his face.

Pete knew immediately that something was up even before he heard the soft, sweet, familiar voice behind him.

"I see the cat's out of the bag."

Pete turned to see Wendy wearing the yellow and pink sundress she'd tried on in Lost Gun. The one that had been too wholesome and sweet for his peace of mind.

His breath caught and it was all he could do not to scoop her up and kiss her for all he was worth.

But something was up and he intended to find out exactly what it was.

"What's Jesse doing here?"

"Making a commercial," she told him. "The commercial you were supposed to make."

"But I signed the papers."

"Because *I* wanted you to." Her words dared him to

deny her and he would have a week ago. "Not because *you* wanted to. You don't want this."

He didn't. But not because he feared it would make him look like a sellout. No, he didn't want it because he wanted her. He wanted to take her back to his ranch and make love and babies.

"You didn't sign them for you," she went on. "And while I appreciate the gesture, I can't let you give up the next three years to do something you don't want to do. So I came up with an alternative plan."

Her eyes twinkled and he remembered the last time he'd seen her. As bittersweet as the moment had been when Red arrived and he'd committed himself to the Western contract, he'd known that she was up to something. He'd just figured she was excited to keep her job and get back to her life.

Instead, she'd been planning something.

"I presented Fred with a new marketing campaign featuring the latest, hottest, wildest bunch on the rodeo circuits." She smiled. "He bought it and the Lost Boys are now the official spokesmen for Outlaw Outfitters."

"So your job is safe."

"Actually, it's not my job anymore. It's Lisa's. She's got plenty of time to deal with everything now that she's officially out of the dating game, waiting on Mr. Right to come to his senses." A smile curved her luscious lips. "I turned in my resignation along with the new ad-campaign proposal."

"I thought you loved Houston."

"I loved the idea of Houston. Of having my own house and painting my own kitchen cabinets and planting roots." Her gaze locked with his. "But I love you more." Sincerity gleamed in her gaze along with a shimmer of insecurity because she'd just poured out her heart to a man who'd professed never to believe in love.

Until now.

"I suppose we could paint *my* kitchen cabinets," he murmured as he pulled her into his arms and held her tight.

"Does that mean you love me?"

"I hate yellow but I'm willing to go with it. Hell, I'll even buy the paint. Does that answer your question?" He pulled back and stared down into her eyes. "I love you, Wendy."

"I love you, too." A serious expression crossed her face and he saw the emotion gleaming in her bright green eyes. "Enough to pack my bags and follow you around if that's what it takes."

"I won't let you do that. I appreciate the offer, but that's not what you want. Hell, it's not what I want. You were right about me. I'm getting tired."

"And old," she reminded him.

"Not that old. Not yet—" He fought down the fear that tightened his throat. "—But I'm getting there. My shoulder hurts like a sonofabitch." He said the words he'd been dreading, and surprisingly the world didn't stop spinning. Instead, it felt as if a weight had lifted off of him. "Grow old with me. We'll go back to my ranch and you can nurse me through a rotator-cuff surgery." He grinned. "Then we'll raise horses and babies."

"And a little hell every now and then?" she added, her lips curving into a smile and her eyes dancing with a passion that scorched him to the quick.

"Every night, sugar," he assured her. "*Every* night."

* * * * *

JULIE LETO

HOOKED

To Kimberly Raye,
for inspiring me to write outside my comfort zone
and to real cowboys everywhere because...
well, do we really need a reason?

1

"YOUR DADDY SURE KNOWS how to make an ass of himself."

James Hooker shut his eyes and gripped his left hand tight to his four-finger pour of bourbon. Hadn't he suffered enough humiliation tonight? He'd had to swallow his pride to accept the peace-offering invitation to Pete Gunner's kid brother's birthday bonfire, never guessing that his own sister would go AWOL and show up on the arm of the man of honor. Or that their father would go ape-shit in front of a crowd of five hundred when he found out.

The bad blood between the Gunners and the Hookers had a long and storied history, but James couldn't be bothered to care. Pete was one of the hottest draws on the circuit. And as the owner of a high-tech arena set to host the next round of Professional Bull Rider events, James didn't need trouble with Pete or the increasingly popular Lost Boys. He wasn't thrilled about his sister flirting around Wade, but his ire had nothing to do with his pompous father's prejudices and everything to do with him not wanting Ginny to make piss-poor decisions just to spite their old man.

He'd been there, done that.

"It's a family trait," he answered, determined not to look at Allie Barrie just yet. Everyone else in town knew better than to throw the sheriff's god-awful behavior in his face—especially when he was tucked into his corner spot at the Marooner's Rock honky-tonk, minding his own business. But his ex, whose voice and perfume he'd recognize if he was blind, deaf and mute, made it her opening salvo.

He took a swig from his glass, but the fiery burn wasn't enough to counteract the way his mouth watered just knowing that Allie was standing less than a foot behind him. He knew it was less than a foot because he could feel the press of her ample breasts against his back—breasts he'd buoyed in his palms, breasts he'd sucked pink and raw, breasts that would make any red-blooded cowboy weep with need.

Allie had that effect on him. Hell, she'd probably have that effect on any man she set her sights on—but she never seemed to look for anyone but him. In the nine years since their breakup, she'd sidled back into town on a manhunt two or three times a year—and he was, as always, her intended prey.

Which was why he'd been avoiding her any way he could.

"You sure left Wade's party right quick," she said. "I didn't even get a chance to ask you to dance."

"I wanted no part of my father's foolishness," he grumbled, swigging down another swallow of whiskey. "Ginny's playing with fire hooking up with that Gunner kid, but the only way she'll learn is to get burned."

"That's the truth. Still, that's an awful philosophical outlook for you, Hook."

He chuckled, but not because her words were funny,

though they were a touch ironic. James had once been a big believer in philosophy—or at least, in a man setting up rules to live by that would keep him on a purposeful path.

Then Allie had come into his life and blown that all to hell.

She snagged his drink, her bare arm snaked slowly past him, teasing him with the scents of sea salt and vanilla. Even though he knew better, he couldn't resist turning his head just enough to watch her slide her tongue along the rim of the glass before she threw back what was left of his bourbon in one bold shot.

"Well, since I've had my fill—" he tipped the brim of his Stetson "—you have yourself a good night."

He swiveled his barstool toward the door, but he'd barely gotten to his feet when she was standing in front of him.

"Don't take off in such a hurry, Hook. The jukebox is humming. How about that dance?"

"I don't dance anymore, Allie."

"Why not? That bull crushed your hand, Hook, not your hips."

His stare seemed enough to force her to change course. His career-ending injury was a sore spot between them. Not the sorest, but close.

"Then we'll just talk," she suggested, her volume rising. Between the chatter of the full-to-capacity bar and the bluegrass music blaring from the jukebox, a private conversation was near to impossible.

But that wouldn't stop her. Nothing stopped her. Nothing but him beating a path to the door.

"You and me don't talk, Allie."

"We used to," she answered, her gulf-green eyes

flashing with determination. "All the time. Remember?"

He squinted, wondering if she'd lost her grip. "Allie, the only time you and I did nothing but talk was when we hadn't yet found out there were a lot more interesting things a boy and girl could do together."

That revelation had come shortly after she'd turned sixteen. Two years later, she'd finally cottoned on to what her classmates had been doing behind the barns during square dances or up in the haylofts when their daddies were off riding cattle or following the circuit. Once she'd figured it out, she'd been insatiable—luckily, just with him.

Until it had all fallen apart.

Nostalgia bent his knees, but even as he moved to sit, he came to his senses and stood again. He was trouble. Allie Barrie was trouble. Together, they were a shitstorm that could wreck even the most secure future plans. He had a mangled hand to prove that much—and a torn-apart life he was only now starting to rebuild.

Not that he'd been sailing around rudderless since she'd packed up for the coast. In nine years, he'd changed course and built a new life for himself. Did he really want to go backward with Allie? Even for just a few minutes?

He was all set to walk out when she dipped her chin. Her long brown hair swept across his shoulders as she turned on the full power of her green eyes. The irises started to swirl in spirals of emerald, jade and pine. He was transfixed. Hypnotized. God almighty, he'd lost hours staring into them once upon a time, watching for that key moment right before the color glazed over and she lost her mind to pleasure. The victorious euphoria that had shot through his system with each of her hard-won orgasms nearly matched the triumph of meeting the requisite eight seconds on the back of a bull.

Nearly.

"Allie, gimme a break. We've talked it all out. Ain't nothing left for us to say to each other."

"That's not true," she insisted. "We haven't talked. You never let me talk! All you do is say that you forgive me and that it wasn't my fault and then you take off. I don't get it, Hook. You don't run from anything. Not two-ton bulls, not your asshole daddy or, hell, not a failing economy into which no one in their right mind would sink their entire future on the off-chance they can turn an old plot of used-up ranch land into something more than dirt. But you run from me. Every damned time."

So, she knew about his latest venture. No big surprise. Lost Gun wasn't a big place and though Allie had moved away for college, she still had plenty of friends and family to keep her informed about the goings-on at the J. Roger Ranch—not to mention the fact that she rarely went more than six months without coming home. He had indeed invested what was left of his savings into transforming the ranch he'd inherited from his uncle into a premiere rodeo destination. However, that fortune hadn't amounted to much more than the land and what was left of his rodeo winnings after he'd paid for business school.

But he had a dream. Well, he had a second dream, his ambition of becoming a top-rated bull rider having gone to hell under the hoof of a two-thousand-pound beast. And he wasn't about to let Allie distract him now by rehashing sins that were best kept in the past.

"I don't run," he said. "But I learn from my mistakes. You and me, we're better off apart. Far apart."

But before he could establish major mileage between her location and his, she snagged him by the sleeve. "That wasn't always true."

"It's true now. More than ever."

"Why? Because when we're together, sparks fly? Sparks that turn into a hot, bone-melting attraction that neither one of us can forget about, even when there are hundreds of miles between us?"

His gut tightened. He didn't want to hurt her again. He'd done his damage when he'd cruelly blamed her for distracting him so that he'd made crucial errors during a ride that had resulted in the destruction of the bones in his right hand. He and Allie were history—and if there was one thing he'd learned from those highfalutin professors at Texas Tech, it was that taking stock of past mistakes was the only way mankind was going to survive.

Hell, it was the only way *he* would survive.

"When we're together, neither one of us can think straight, that much is true. But I need my head right now. I've got a lot going on and the last person I want around is you."

WHEN JAMES HOOKER MEANT to hurt, he didn't miss. His words sliced through her like a blade, stunning her into shocked stillness long enough for him to mutter an unconvincing, "Sorry," toss a couple of bills on the bar and disappear into the night.

Or at least, disappear into the parking lot. Allie had endured enough of the man's whetted barbs to recover quickly. So he was angry with her. That was nothing new. Ever since that first outburst hours after the doctors had declared his hand unrepairable, he'd made himself scarce whenever she was around. On the few times she'd managed to corner him, he'd claimed that he no longer blamed her for her part in the destruction of what might have been a long, profitable career.

But he had never been very convincing and Allie had had enough of his dismissive assurances. They'd been inseparable nearly their whole lives, first as friends, then as first-love lovers. The rails around the ring where he'd ridden his first bull probably still had the permanent nail marks, just like the spot below her right hip bone still had a miniscule tattoo he'd bought her for her seventeenth birthday—a sideways number eight.

He'd said it was to commemorate the miraculous eight seconds it took for a cowboy to reach nirvana, but she'd known better. It was the symbol of infinity—the eternity they might have spent together if she hadn't gotten pregnant.

When she'd seen the pink line, she'd freaked. She hadn't thought about how springing the news on him right before a ride might mess with his head. His legendary concentration shot to hell, he'd made a rookie error. He'd been bucked off hard and the bull had crushed Hook's hand.

That had been a long time ago. Since then, she'd gone to college, gotten a degree in marine biology, a master's in marine ecosystem dynamics and was one dissertation away from her doctorate in the same. Her graduate advisor had recommended her for a once-in-a-lifetime job at an eco-friendly marine-themed hotel in the Caribbean—a sweet offer she just couldn't bring herself to take just yet.

Not when James Hooker still occupied parts of her soul.

But that's precisely why she'd delayed accepting. Despite the half-dozen messages Dr. Eric Rayburn had

left for her, she'd eschewed the summer-break fun in
Port Aransas in order to come back home and put her
feelings for Hook to rest.

She slapped through the honky-tonk's hokey double doors and headed straight toward Hook's beat-up
Ford truck. She'd parked right next to him. She wished
she'd thought to block him in, but she wouldn't put it
past Hook to simply roll his four-wheel drive right over
her cute little convertible coupe in his haste to escape.

Instead, she whistled in the way her daddy'd taught
her.

"We're not done!"

When his back taillights flashed, she jogged the rest
of the distance, launched herself onto the running board
and slapped her palm on the driver's-side window.

"I'm not kidding around this time, Hook. I'm not
leaving until we put this bad blood behind us."

He rolled down the window and cursed. "Why are
you doing this to me, Allie?"

The fact that he hadn't just driven off, forcing her
to either jump clear or hang on for dear life, gave her
enough hope to tease him with a smile, despite her flip-
flopping stomach.

"Doing what?"

"You wanna talk or you wanna flirt?"

"I remember when you loved that I could do both."

"That was a hell of a long time ago," he said, his
finger pointed for emphasis. "I'm not going back there.
And neither should you."

"Why not? You can't say you haven't missed me."

"I haven't missed you."

The muscle in his chin twitched.

"Liar."

"Don't do this, Allie."

"What? Offer you a taste of what you haven't had in a ridiculously long time?"

"Is that what you think you're doing? I don't know what you've heard, Allie, but I'm making out just fine."

"Making out? With who? Connie Parker? She's a prude. If she's putting out, it's just until she gets a ring on her finger and then she'll cut you off. Or maybe Lynette Swank? I hear she's always anxious to do the deed, but comes so easy that a guy just has to wiggle a little finger in her direction and the fun's over. I'm not like that, am I, Hook? I'm a challenge—one you were always up to the task of facing. And now I'm back for who knows how long, acting like a fool in some crazy hope that we can put things right between us."

"*Crazy* is the word," he muttered.

"Crazy. Determined. Take your pick. But either way, I'm not giving up. Once I set my mind to something, I'm unstoppable—and you know it. I'm going to be your shadow, dogging your every step, until you give me what I want."

"What do you really want, Allie, forgiveness? Hell, woman. I told you. I already gave you that. Years ago. Let it go, already."

"That's not what I want. Not anymore."

"What do you want, then? Tell me and I swear to God, I'll give it to you in a heartbeat if it means you'll leave me the hell alone."

"Promise?"

He crossed his heart with his finger.

"Okay," she said, deciding to call his bluff. She slid sideways along the running board, flipped open his door and climbed in like she used to, settling on his lap. "I want a baby."

2

JAMES DIDN'T KNOW what shocked him more—the feel
of Allie's sweet body contouring to his or the fact that
she'd just asked for the one thing he knew she didn't
want, or need.

"You don't mean that," he said.

"H-how do you know what I mean?"

She was shaking, damn her. Every emotion rippling
through her body was injected into him. Fear. Shock.
Regret.

Attraction.

From the first minute he'd stolen a kiss on her daddy's back porch, he'd known that her chemistry and
his worked together like fire and sulfur. Every patient
fiber in his teenage body had been tested as they'd
progressed from the sweet pressing of lips to tongue-
tangling French kisses to sneaking touches beneath her
T-shirt and beyond, culminating in the triumphant moment when he'd finally coaxed her to slide her hand
down the waistband of his jeans.

That had been the night they'd first made love. As
if holding his hard sex had broken the last barriers of
her resistance, she'd wanted him inside her—and once

there, he'd discovered a silky piece of heaven that even today, after all that had happened, he wanted to explore again.

But he wasn't a hormone-driven kid anymore. He was a man who knew that messing around with Allie would lead to nothing good for either of them.

"You don't want a baby," he said. "Least of all with me."

"Why not with you? Wasn't that our plan for all those years? Wasn't that what almost happened? We were so close. If only I hadn't—"

Mustering the full breadth of his self-control, James eased Allie off of his lap and onto the passenger seat, cutting her off before she talked about things that didn't need to be rehashed. She'd gotten pregnant with his child. She'd lost the baby to a miscarriage. Didn't mean they had any business trying again.

He shoved the truck into Park and turned off the ignition. It was a hot night, but even the soft hum of the engine sounded like a bluegrass band jangling in his ears. Living in the past—even thinking about those old fantasies or painful disappointments—dug up a septic tank's worth of a deep, dark rage he preferred to flush away, along with his aspirations at rodeo titles, endless glory and endorsement deals.

Shit happened. Riders got hurt—sometimes so bad, there was no means of recovery. He'd come to terms with his new ambitions a long time ago. But Allie, she held fast to those old dreams like one of his dogs might to a side of beef. When he'd spied Allie at the Gunners' shindig, he'd had a vague idea that at some point during the night, he'd have to either elude her or deal yet again with her unshakeable desire to rekindle a relationship that had gone south a long time ago.

But never in a million years had he dreamed they'd be talking like this—about the very heart of the tragedy that had ripped them apart.

"Plans change," he said, and in a moment of pure spite, he raised his right hand.

The fingers worked. Barely. His joints ached all the damned time. His knuckles resembled the coins he used to feed into a machine at the fair that stamped scenes from the Alamo onto the squashed copper, only the impressions on his crushed bones were the leftover scars from the hooves of a two-thousand-pound bull.

Allie scooted away from him. The light from the nearby streetlamp streamed into the cab of the truck, catching the glossy sheen in her eyes. Damn. He dropped his hand into the shadows, then turned to reach toward her with his left.

"Allie, don't."

She shoved his good hand aside. "Don't what? Don't feel bad that I caused you so much pain? Wrecked your career?"

"You didn't wreck my career. A bull named Hell's Vengeance did that."

"I shouldn't have told you about the baby right before you got on that bull. I should have waited."

"No, I shouldn't have loaded into that chute when I didn't have my head on straight. And I should have used better condoms."

He shifted so that he was facing forward, but out of the corner of his eye, he saw Allie's hand drift to her belly. Earlier, when her lacy blouse had ridden up as she stretched across a buffet table to snag a handful of chips, he noticed the skin there was still flat and taut. He shouldn't have been watching her that way—shouldn't have let old memories of dipping his tongue into her belly button and below snake back into his brain. He shouldn't have even noticed that she was among the hundreds who had paraded out to the Gunner place to celebrate Wade's big day—but he had. Allie didn't come around often, but when she did, he knew.

Not because of the gossip around town. Not because of the way his father got grumpier or his sister got extra quiet. He knew because Allie's heartbeat seemed connected to his so that he could hear it thrumming in his ears whenever she was within a ten-mile radius.

And right now, it was beating like a bass drum.

"See what I mean, Allie? We're together less than ten minutes and I'm hurting you in a way that's not right after all this time. I try to give you a wide berth when you come back home. But you keep hunting me down when you know it's a bad idea."

"It doesn't have to be," she said, a plea in her voice. "If we could just get beyond the hurt from the past, maybe we'll find something new. I know it sounds desperate. Maybe even pathetic. But I can't get you out of my mind whether I'm here or in Port Aransas or anywhere else I might go. I have to figure out why that is, Hook, and dammit, I can't unless you let me in."

His chest constricted so tight, he felt as if he'd been roped around the middle. They had left a lot of things unsaid and unresolved. In his bid to put the past behind him, he had left too many wounds unhealed.

Physically, both of them had bounced back. But what about the wounds underneath the skin and bone and muscle?

"You don't want something new with me, Allie. You want what we had before everything fell apart. Well, we can't have that. Neither one of us. We aren't. kids anymore."

"No, we aren't. That's the beauty of it. We're adults. We know what we're getting ourselves into. Know that in the end, things might not work out. But we also know that the risk might be worth it."

He didn't know how she'd managed, but Allie had pushed all of the sadness out of her voice. She'd always had an amazing capacity to bounce back from disappointment, whether it was the time she'd lost her bid to be head cheerleader because her calculus grade had been below standards or when she'd been denied a shot at a summer internship at Sea World in Austin because her father didn't want her living so far from home. Allie had always found a way to turn her tragedy into triumph.

Hell, even losing him and his baby hadn't stopped her from running off to college and getting her first degree a year ahead of schedule—a fact he remembered with a hell of a lot more resentment than he wanted to feel.

Maybe he did have some residual emotions he needed to work out, but that was best done when she was far, far away.

"I gotta go," he said. "I got a meeting with my business partners tomorrow, and if I was a betting man, I'd expect that sometime in the middle of the night, Ginny is either going to show up at my door begging for sanctuary against my father's tirades or I'm going to get an emergency call to go back home and break up their latest battle."

The tension ebbed as the subject changed to his suddenly feisty sibling. Allie grinned as if prouder than punch that Ginny had showed some gumption around blustery J. R. Hooker. "I can't believe she stood up to him earlier."

James shook his head, a grin busting through at the thought that his usually meek little sister had finally shown a streak of Hooker strength. "Neither can I. That's why I didn't step in, to be truthful. Figured she was doing just fine on her own and it's about time she learned to deal with our old man on her own terms."

"She's growing up," Allie said brightly. "Facing the rough stuff is what being an adult is about."

James groaned, but couldn't suppress his smile. The woman was, in addition to still beautiful, stubborn and single-minded as hell.

"First, you tell me you didn't come back here specifically to get knocked up," he insisted.

Maybe he owed her a chance to work him out of her system—and vice versa. But that was his limit.

"I didn't," she confessed. "I swear. Well, I mean, I do want a baby. Sooner rather than later. But I didn't come home to get pregnant. I just want to move on with my life and I can't seem to do that until you and I settle things. And it's not going to happen in one brief conversation. We have too much history. Too much hurt. Too much leftover lust."

He wanted to deny the last part, but he couldn't. Despite all his pent-up anger and resentment, she still made his heart race. If she asked if he still dreamed about the hot nights they'd spent in the back of his pickup, he'd be lying if he said no. The memories didn't haunt him every night, but they disrupted his sleep often enough for him to accept that he wasn't quite as over her as he wanted her to believe.

"You staying at your dad's?"

She shook her head. "His new wife turned my old room into quilting-and-crafting central about a month after she moved in. Aunt Maylene gave me the keys to

the apartment over the diner again. She decided rent-
ers were too much trouble and doesn't do much with it
now except save it for me when I visit. But to be honest, I kind of wanted to see your new place."

"Not much to see in the dead of night," he countered.

"There's always the morning."

Gripping the steering wheel tightly with his good
hand, James took a deep breath. This was almost like
being on the back of a bull again. Around him, there
was madness. Bright lights, loud noise, voices of his
teammates shouting orders, trying to keep the bull at
the right angle so that when the chute opened, he'd have
a better chance at keeping his seat. But in that second
before the pick-up man pulled open the gate, Hook had
always tried to find the silence—the communal moment when no one but him and the bull existed. Man
and beast. Life and death.

Now, it was just him and Allie. The past snorted and
scuffed and bucked beneath them and until they mas-
tered the ride, neither of them would find any victory—
or any peace.

"You want to follow me out or leave your car?" he
asked, resigned.

She wiggled in her seat. "And let the whole town start
speculating about where I disappeared to if I leave my
car in the lot? No, thanks. I'll follow you."

She popped out of the cab and jogged around the
back, her sports car roaring to life seconds later. He
turned the ignition and waited for her to back out before he threw the truck into Reverse. If she left her car
in the parking lot of Marooner's Rock, no one in Lost
Gun would have to speculate about where she was.
They'd all guess that she'd gone home with him—and

for some reason that made absolutely no sense, that pleased him.

More than it should have.

ALLIE DROVE IN A DAZE. Luckily, traversing the paved back roads around Lost Gun didn't require much thought. As long as she kept her eyes focused on the bright red taillights of James's pickup, she'd get where she was going.

The question was—what was she going to do once she got there?

She'd planned for this. She had an overnight bag in the backseat that she'd put together precisely for this contingency. She had makeup, her toothbrush, a supply of condoms, sexy lingerie, high-heeled, do-me-quick shoes and a change of clothes for the morning so that her walk of shame wouldn't be quite so obvious to anyone who might be taking note of her comings and goings.

But she hadn't expected to open her heart so widely in order to get her here. A baby? Since when? Okay, so she was keenly aware that she wasn't getting any younger. And since her breakup with James, no man in her life had come even close to sparking her need to nest and procreate. Less than ten minutes in his presence and the most innate, most basic needs that she'd suppressed for a decade had bubbled to the surface— or had they?

All the times she'd pictured James and her finally hooking up again, it had been all about seduction, passion and undeniable need. She'd sashay past him at just the right moment, wearing a spritz of the perfume he'd liked back in high school and he'd drop all the drama from their past, sweep her into his arms and make wild love to her on the flatbed of his truck.

That scenario might still play out—but not without a price.

The price of confession.

The price of repentance.

The price of truth.

Each separately, she might be able to afford. But together? All at once?

She exhaled, not realizing she'd been holding her breath until her lungs had started to ache. Well, Allie Barrie, you started this. You've been after him for years, chasing him down like a shameless buckle bunny every time you came home from school. Now you've got him—what are you going to do? Run away from the very tempest you've stirred?

No, she wouldn't run. She had to do this—had either to find her way back into James Hooker's heart or burn his imprint out of her own ticker for good. And the baby thing? She'd have to take her time on that one, figure out if she'd been covering up that need for a long time or if her desire to reconnect with James had short-circuited her brain.

Her cell phone chirped. Very few people had her cell-phone number and since the timing was impeccable, she wasn't surprised to see her best friend's name flash on the screen.

"Well?"

"I found him," Allie replied.

"And?"

"I'm following him now."

Samantha Gibson, the first college roommate who hadn't driven her crazy by stealing her clothes or sneaking her boyfriend into their dorm room at two in the morning, clucked her tongue. "Do we need to have that little conversation about stalking again, sweetie? Because there's a fine line between true love and crazy, bat-shit obsession."

Allie chuckled. Sam always did cut to the heart of the matter, even when it was damned inconvenient. It was one of the reasons they were so compatible and had stuck to rooming together since sophomore year. It helped that they'd ended up in the same course of study, both determined to save the world by starting with the oceans.

"Is it stalking if he knows I'm following him? I didn't want to leave my car in the parking lot of the honky-tonk. People around here like to talk."

"What the hell else do they have to do with their time out in the middle of frickin' nowhere?" Miami-born and bred, Sam considered any and all Texas towns as beneath her cosmopolitan tastes, except Austin, maybe, because of the overabundance of universities. Only her unshakeable interest in the preservation of marine life in the Gulf of Mexico kept her in Port Aransas—along with its relative proximity to Corpus Christi, which was city enough in a pinch. But she'd declined all of Allie's invitations to join her in Lost Gun, somehow afraid that she'd lose her taste for mojitos and Jimmy Choos and would end up chugging beer out of a red plastic cup and wearing Wranglers.

"Trust me, we have plenty of good stuff to do here in Lost Gun."

"Which is clearly why you're following him home. You sure he's leading you somewhere safe and not to some far-out pasture where we won't find your body until next spring?"

"James is a lover, not a fighter."

"I thought he was a bull rider."

"They ride the bulls, they don't kill them. We're going back to his place. To talk."

"Uh-huh," Sam replied, her doubt coming through loud and clear in two muttered syllables.

But Allie didn't try to convince her otherwise. If one thing led to another and she ended up in James Hooker's bed, she wasn't going to fight it. Over the years, she couldn't count the number of times she'd tried to get this far with him. He'd always eluded her. Sometimes, he went out of town. Sometimes, he only showed his face at crowded events where he had friends and family so close, they didn't get a moment alone. A few times, he'd even clung to women who were totally wrong for him, knowing that Allie would never be so rude as to insert herself into his space if he was on a date.

This time, however, she'd caught him alone and vulnerable. She wasn't about to pass up this rare opportunity just because her best friend thought she'd lost her mind.

"Why are you checking up on me, anyway? You usually don't even like calling me when I'm here as if you're afraid you're going to pick up my accent."

"It does get more pronounced when you go back. You know that, right?"

"I reckon it does," she drawled, half teasing. "It's a small price to pay."

"It's going to be a bigger price if you let a certain job opportunity pass you by. Dr. Rayburn called again. He wants your cell-phone number, but I told him you'd expressly forbidden me from giving it out to anyone, even to the man who wants to make you his assistant at the most cutting-edge marine facility the world has ever seen. He made me promise to give you a message."

Allie pressed her lips together. Did she really want to

know what Eric had to say? He'd been sweetening the pot in his attempts to lure her to his new project—and hinting that once he was no longer her doctorate advisor, he might want to take their so-far-purely-academic relationship a personal step further.

He was handsome. And intelligent. And persistent. But none of that mattered when she wasn't even sure what she wanted to do once she had her doctorate—and not just because of her unfinished business with James.

"Do I want to hear his message?" she asked.

"Depends on how bad you want that cowboy."

"I want him to the depths of my soul," Allie replied.

"Then I'll call you tomorrow and give you Rayburn's message. You concentrate on working that man out of your system so you can get back here and start fresh."

"Or not," Allie said.

Finally Samantha stopped her grumbling and said nothing more than goodbye. Allie clicked the phone off just as James took a right-hand turn onto the dirt road that would lead them to his place. Once there, Allie had no idea what was going to happen—but she had a strong feeling that by morning, she'd know one way or another whether she was going to keep up her pursuit of James Hooker or if she was finally ready to let him go.

3

JAMES PARKED IN FRONT of the house, leaving room on the gravel drive for Allie to ease her car to a stop behind him. Several times during the ride home, he'd thought about making a U-turn and guiding her back to town where she belonged—but then he realized she didn't really belong there, either.

She had a life in Port Aransas, according to her father. She'd gotten bachelor's and master's degrees from the Marine Institute at the University of Texas and was nearly done with a doctorate. He'd also heard that she'd been offered some kind of fancy job at a private aquarium, though the local gossip hadn't provided much by way of details, probably because Allie kept them close to the vest. Either way, Allie was moving up and moving on—and yet, every time she came home, she made it her business to hunt him down.

Now, she'd caught him. That he'd finally let her get close enough to lock her chompers onto his heart again told him more about himself than he wanted to know.

As much as he'd thought he was done with her, he wasn't—not by a long shot.

He locked up the truck and went around back in time to see her pulling an overnight bag out of her backseat.

"You came prepared," he commented.

She slammed her door and shouldered the bag. "Like a Scout."

He held out a hand. "I don't think the little girls who sell cookies door to door would be happy to have you as a spokeswoman, knowing what you've come prepared for."

"You have no idea what I'm willing to do with you, James Hooker," she countered.

He snatched her bag, plopped it on top of the hood of her car and unzipped the top. She opened her mouth to protest, but stopped herself and crossed her arms instead. He didn't have to dig in far to find what he was looking for—and once he did, he was half-sorry he had.

But only half. His other half desperately wanted to see her strut across his bedroom with the mile-high spiked shoes on her feet.

He wolf-whistled loud enough that he heard his dogs bark in response from somewhere in the south field.

She snagged the shoe out of his hand and shoved it back inside her bag. "Don't make me regret coming here," she warned.

"Sweetheart, if you don't already regret it, then you aren't going to. What do you want to see first? The new building or the house?"

She slung the bag back onto her shoulder. "What do you think?"

He started toward the house.

In the pink glow of the porch light, James noticed that he hadn't done much to clear up the front of his house since he'd inherited it from his uncle. He usually parked around back and couldn't remember the last time he'd gone inside through the main entrance. The old rockers with their peeling paint and cracked back slats sagged under the weight of rusted tools, battered boots and rotted ropes he'd been meaning to toss out. The floorboards creaked under their weight and he was sure if he allowed himself a few minutes to notice when the sun was up, the whole place needed a new coat of paint.

But his priorities had been elsewhere—on fulfilling the responsibility he'd been left when Uncle Deke had willed the place to him rather than to his own son.

Luckily for James, his cousin Paul, a big-time lawyer in Houston, had welcomed the idea. He was just happy that someone would put the old place to good use. He'd even invested heavily in James's project—a dream his uncle had had for more years than he could remember, though the old wrangler hadn't had the business acumen to turn a good idea into reality.

The J. Roger Ranch had long been a destination for new blood looking to learn about riding, roping and rodeoing. A former champion himself, Deke Hooker had trained up the next generation of wranglers for years, all while keeping a small herd or two of cattle and horses to pay the bills. He'd eventually sold off all the animals except the ones he used for training and by the time a series of heart attacks finally took the life hundreds of bulls and broncos had failed to slow, a tradition of the J. Roger hosting smaller competitions had taken root. Structures had been erected for shade, bleachers had been built to sustain crowds and an old brick barbecue had been turned into a concession stand that could feed anyone and everyone who traveled to Lost Gun to watch the cowboys hone their craft.

But Deke had wanted more. He'd dreamed of turning the J. Roger into a premiere destination for the official PBR competitions, and after James had graduated from business school, he'd done everything to help his uncle realize the dream. Thanks to the investors Paul had found, James was putting the finishing touches on a slick new arena. And since his money men were coming to visit tomorrow to check on the progress, he should have been spending the evening making sure everything was spit-shined and ready.

But he'd tend to that in the morning. Tonight, the only thing he was going to work on was making sure that at some point, he saw Allie in those shoes.

Just inside the door, he flipped on a lamp, then backed up so Allie could enter first. She walked slowly, as if she was strolling into some kind of museum rather than the place he'd called home for the past couple of years.

"Place hasn't changed much," she commented.

James had always been close to his Uncle Deke, so Allie had spent a good deal of time with him here back when he was training.

"Deke left me the whole ranch, but I'd been bunking in the back since his first heart attack."

"I was sorry to hear he died," she said. "I know you were close. And he was always real decent to me, even when he thought I was a distraction to your training regimen."

James chuckled. His uncle had never been anything but kind to Allie, but he'd complained more than a few times in private that James shouldn't have a girlfriend if he was serious about competing. It must have taken every ounce of his self-control not to throw his warnings in his nephew's face after the accident. But he hadn't. Not once.

"He was a good man. Calm. Fluid in his ideas about right and wrong."

"In other words, the polar opposite of your father."

He nodded, then took off his Stetson and ran his hand through his hair. "That pretty much sums it up. I haven't had time to change much around here just yet, but it's a place to hang my hat."

"It could be more than that," she said, looking around with assessing eyes. "With the right touches."

He supposed she was right, but he couldn't see why anyone would bother. The house had a homey, warm atmosphere left over from when his aunt had been alive. She'd been a simple woman with no need for anything that hadn't been in her family for generations. Other than pictures above the mantel of his cousin Paul transforming from chubby-cheeked baby to law-school graduate, the whole place looked as if it was stuck in time.

Once he was a widower, Deke hadn't cared enough to change anything, and now that he was gone, James figured he'd keep things just the same, too. Wasn't like he spent much time in the parlor anyway. Even now that he lived here alone, he tended to keep to the kitchen, his bedroom and the back side of the wraparound porch.

And of those three locations, he knew exactly which one he wanted to show Allie next.

"My room's through there," he said, gesturing down the long hall.

He flipped on a hall light just in time to spy the hesitation in her step.

"Unless you've changed your mind?"

Her determined gaze locked with his. "About being here? Not on your life. I just feel like I've finally entered the inner sanctum and I'm not sure if I need to make a sign of the cross or genuflect or something."

He gave her a playful shove in the direction of his room. "You always were overly dramatic."

"Me? Remember that time you snuck me into your room when your daddy was out arresting Billy Sumter for taking a bath in the water trough outside the Burning Bear tack shop?"

A rush of heat suffused his face and he was glad for the relative darkness. He'd done some really stupid things in his teenage years, but the way he'd reacted to his father coming home unexpectedly after he'd snuck Allie into his room for a little afternoon delight had to top the list.

"Who would have guessed old Billy would go along quietly and Pops would be home an hour and a half sooner than either of us expected?"

She laughed. "I was buck-naked and about five minutes away from a soul-shattering orgasm when you heard his car pull into the garage. I nearly died of shock right there across your bed."

"If he'd have caught you, we would have been the ranch version of Romeo and Juliet—two young lovers dead before their time. Luckily, I'm a quick thinker."

"You threw me into the closet!"

"Good thing you darted out and folded up inside that old trunk next to my bed instead. He beelined straight for the closet once he realized I was home and half-dressed instead of at the movies."

She slid her hand to the small of her back and stretched. "I was nice and limber then."

"And you're not now?"

They'd reached the end of the hall. His door was wide open. The moonlight streaming in from the windows on either side of his bed illuminated what he suddenly hoped would be their final destination.

Allie dropped her bag just inside the door, but didn't go in.

"I guess we'll find out soon enough. Where's the lady's room in this man cave?"

He could have directed her to his bathroom, but he wasn't sure he'd picked up since he lit out of the house earlier. Instead, he sent her to the guest bathroom near the kitchen. With a curse that kept him from feeling like he was a teenager again, he darted inside his room, picked up a few stray socks that belonged in the hamper and silently thanked Sarah, his housekeeper, for changing the sheets only a day ago. In the bathroom, he shoved his razor and aftershave into the medicine cabinet and flattened out the damp towel he'd thrown over the top of the shower rod.

He tried to remember the last time he'd brought a woman home with him and realized that he hadn't. At least, not since he'd moved in to his uncle's place. Didn't seem right when the man was alive, and even after he'd gone, James had protected his space from feminine invasion. He certainly hadn't been a monk, but when he spent time with a woman, he'd end up at her place, not his, something he hadn't realized until Allie stood in the doorway and cleared her throat.

"This looks like you," she said.

He glanced around. The room didn't have much in it besides a king-size bed with a patchwork comforter, a leather easy chair he'd brought with him from his college apartment, a couple of dressers for his clothes and plenty of lamps for reading. On the walls, he'd hung his sheepskin from Texas A&M, a trio of pictures from his rodeo days and a collage of him with Ginny, his mom, and even one from his high-school graduation, standing beside his dad, whose genuine, straight-to-the-bone grin made it apparent he hadn't expected his oldest child to make it all the way through to the ceremony.

"It's a place to sleep," he replied.

She sauntered into the room, swinging her hips in that subtle, sweet little way that he'd forever associate with Allie Barrie.

"Is that all it's a place for?"

"Up until now," he answered.

She chuckled. "You want me to believe you've never had a woman...or twelve, here before now?"

"Have you ever known me to be a player?"

Allie's heart thumped an extra couple of beats. She knew from her own personal experience that despite the fact that James Hooker was the hottest guy in the whole state of Texas, he'd been faithful to her for the entire four years that they had been together.

Four years. Damn, it had felt like a decade, but they'd now spent twice as much time apart as they had together. She knew he'd had a few lovers since she'd left for school. She hadn't been celibate, either, though her interludes had been few and far between and never more serious than a girl needed them to be so she wouldn't feel guilty about letting a man into her bed.

But had he really never brought anyone home?

"You don't have to be a player to share that big bed with someone."

"I'm not big on sharing," he replied. "Most women whom I hook up with don't want to wait long enough to drive all the way out here to get what they want."

She laughed as she rolled her eyes, acknowledging both the truth and the exaggeration of his claim. "That I can buy."

"But you don't seem to have any trouble waiting for what you want," he said, shoving his hat onto a spike by the door and then sitting down on the corner of his mattress. "You seem to have endless supplies of patience."

"Got me here after all these years, didn't it?"

"That it did. And now that you've made it, are you going to stay sheltered in the doorway as if you're expecting an earthquake or are you going to come on in and get what you came for?"

Again, he cut right to the chase. And again, the nerve endings radiating from the deepest part of her trembled in response. Allie pushed off from the doorjamb, but wasn't exactly sure where to go next. She wanted to slide onto his lap and kiss the challenging look right off his face, but she had too much riding on tonight to make the wrong move. If there was one thing she knew for sure, it was that the sexual tension spiking between James and her wasn't going anywhere—if it hadn't lessened in nearly nine years, it wasn't going to disperse in ten minutes.

Unless, of course, the unspoken truths zapped it all to hell.

She settled into the well-worn chair beside his window. Snuggling her backside into the James-size indentation, she inhaled the scent of the leather and what she suspected might be hints of his shampoo or aftershave.

"How much did you hate me after I left?" she asked.

His bright blue eyes widened for a second, as if she'd shocked him by asking a question rather than turning up the heat. Well, it wasn't the last time tonight she was going to his push limits...or hers.

"More than I wanted to," he said.

"What did you want instead?"

"To forget I ever knew you," he replied. "No offense, Allie, but I was hurt. Physically and—well, deeper than that. If I could have turned back time, I would have."

"I know," she acknowledged. The combined agony of losing the only man she'd ever loved and the baby that they'd made together had nearly knocked her unconscious. The miscarriage, unexpected and never explained, had thrown her into a spiral of despair she'd never thought she'd survive. But being raised by a single father had taught her that wallowing in her sadness wasn't going to change anything. She could have stayed in Lost Gun and tortured herself with Hook's righteous anger or she could take the early admission to college and see if moving away could lessen the pain.

It had, to some degree. But the longer she stayed at school, the deeper she suppressed her emotions until they finally bubbled to the surface and demanded she work them out. She'd been trying to do that for years with James, but he'd never given her a chance.

Until now.

"Every time I came home, I tried to talk to you. Work things out. Put the past to rest. You wouldn't listen."

He cursed even as he nodded in agreement. "When all this shit went down, Allie, I was nineteen years old. In the course of one month, I learned I was going to be a daddy, then that I'd lost my chance at ever riding a bull again, and then that you'd lost the baby. What was I supposed to think? To feel?"

"Angry," she said, resigned. Without a doubt, that month had been the worst of her entire life. In the time it took for her to sneak a pregnancy test out of her father's drug store and get the shocking results, the future she'd planned on with James had imploded. He wanted to ride the circuit for a while, save up his winnings, buy a piece of his uncle's ranch and build them a house with a hot tub where he could soak his tired muscles. She'd planned to go to college, maybe study to be a biology teacher or some other profession that would keep her from getting lonely when James was on the road for the season, racking up points and profits.

But one little pink plus sign had changed everything.

She'd been so terrified. With no mother to run to and no girlfriends who valued loyalty over gossip, she'd run straight to the one person she could trust—James.

"But you weren't angry when I first told you," she reminded him.

He drove his hands through his hair again, setting the pitch-black locks on end in a way that made her fingers ache to set right.

"I was too shocked. A baby. Me, nineteen. You, seventeen. All I could think about was how scared you were. You came to me for reassurance. Protection. I didn't want to let you down."

"You didn't," she said, launching off the chair. She slid beside him on the bed, close enough to experience the intoxication of his scent, but not his body heat, though the warmth teased the edge of her awareness.

So close. So spiced with musk and leather and man.

"You were good to me, James. In that crazy moment when I was more terrified than I'd been in my entire life, I knew things were going to work out because you said so. I wasn't scared. Not until that chute opened and everything—"

"—I don't want to relive that," he said, shaking his head. "I don't remember much, anyway. Just the pain."

He stretched his mangled hand and for the first time since he and Allie had ended their relationship, she slid her long, strong fingers over his scarred, mangled ones.

He flinched, but didn't pull away.

"Does it still hurt?" she asked.

"Only when it's going to rain."

She glided her fingers into the spaces between his, her palm nestling over the hand he'd hurt because she'd allowed her own selfish fears to override every ounce of good sense the good Lord had given her.

She should have waited until after his ride. She should have held her own terror in check long enough for James to ride that bull, qualify for the next level, and pocket his winnings. How differently would things have turned out if she'd just kept her mouth shut for another half an hour, maybe less?

"Feel any precipitation in our future?" she asked, sliding her other hand beneath his so that she'd sandwiched his warmth with hers. Touching him now, as it had in the past, fascinated her. Something about the way his skin felt against hers wrapped her up in a cocoon of curiosity and intrigue—as if every sensation was a mystery that needed to be fully explored.

When he answered, his voice was as low and as rumbling as thunder. "I have a strong premonition that things are about to get real wet, real soon."

She lifted her gaze to his, not at all surprised to see brazen lust zigzagging across his blue-sky irises like the lightning. But this tempest wasn't going to hurt them. It would heal them. She knew it. She'd stake her future on it. And his.

4

JAMES KNEW ALLIE was going to kiss him. He watched her eyes, so green and hypnotic, cloud over with that familiar fog of need that helped a woman do things that might not seem so right if she had complete clarity.

But he wasn't going to stop her. He was a man who knew when to put up his dukes and when to surrender to the inevitable. Since she'd left, he'd been on guard, perpetually looking over his shoulder, trying to protect himself from the dangers of tangling with any woman who might chomp down on his heart—and Allie Barrie was the most ravenous of all. And yet, the moment her sweet, slick lips pressed lightly to his, every ounce of tension holding his body upright melted away.

He wanted this. He wanted her. He'd rather take a death roll with her into the depths of dangerous desire than continue sailing away from trouble—safe, but unchallenged. He needed this. He needed her.

"Allie," he breathed as she pressed their tangled hands against his chest until he was lying flat on his back.

"Tell me you don't want me," she challenged, her

body stretched out across his so that her breasts nestled against him, her pelvis flush with his.

"I won't lie to you."

"Then lie with me," she begged. "I'm not asking for more than just tonight. One night. By morning, we'll know what's left, if anything, between us. I need to know, James. I can't move on when I'm still so rooted in the past."

He shook his head, even as she trailed her lips across the curve of his jaw then up to the lobe of his ear. Groans of pleasure plucked through his brain while she traced the sensitive skin with her tongue, her strong left hand still twined with his weakened right one. In some dark part of his heart that was too damned deep for him to reach when the soft weight of her ample breasts blocked the route, he knew they shouldn't do this. Making love with Allie was going to open him up to troubles he'd left behind him years ago.

But then, maybe opening up those troubles would finally set them free.

He flipped her over, instantly invigorated by the familiar feel of her body beneath his. Her breath caught, but a smile lit her eyes like green fire.

"You're sure?" he asked.

"I've never been more sure of anything in my whole life," she said.

That was all he needed to know. This time, he did the kissing, plundering her mouth with all the vigor of a seventeen-year-old boy and the skill of a twenty-nine-year-old man who'd parted those lips before, who'd tangled tongues with her more times than he could count and who had intoxicated himself on her flavors so often, everything about her was familiar and fresh at the same time. She tore at the buttons of his shirt while he lifted the hem of hers and in what seemed like a flash of fabric and lace, they were bare from the waist up.

Her tan lines made him rock hard. Her breasts, full and lush, were pale triangles outlined by darker flesh that matched the centers of her areolas. She spent enough time in the sun to turn her nipples into bull's-eyes—ones he didn't intend to miss.

He ran his damaged hand up from her waist, then over her breasts. The hard flesh of his scars scraped over her silky softness until it met the bud. He didn't have a lot of strength in his joints, but his nerve endings worked just fine. He reveled in the dense weight of her, in her satin texture, in her open responsiveness that had her panting and cooing with each flick of his thumb over the sensitive nub.

She grabbed the sides of his cheeks and met him halfway in a kiss that was sloppy and hungry and honest and desperate and real—so real, it beat away the last of his old fantasies and gave him a clarity he hadn't had for a long time.

The dim lamp on his bedside was insufficient for the moment. He rolled off her, kissing her softly on the tip of her nose before he pulled down the blinds and turned on every light in the room, including the one in the bathroom.

"Are you sending some kind of signal to the electric company?" she asked, a giggle in her voice.

"Nope," he said, toeing out of his boots before he unbuckled his belt and unzipped his jeans. "I just don't want to miss an inch of you. My one hand might not be what it used to, but my eyes work just fine. Better than fine."

She snagged her bottom lip in her teeth. "I don't think we ever made love in this much light before."

He dropped his pants. "Unless you count sunlight. Remember that one time? In the south pasture? Up near the creek?"

Her cheeks pinkened. Of course she remembered. She'd worn a frilly little sundress that afternoon—and no panties. It had been the first time she'd allowed him to taste her down there, his head buried beneath the cottony folds of her skirt.

"How could I forget?"

He hummed his agreement, then stepped out of his boxers, leaving himself open to her widening gaze. Scars aside, he had a lot to be proud of, so he remained still until her stare reached his jutting sex.

She licked her lips.

Oh, yeah. He was going to feel those lips wrapped around him at some point tonight, but that wasn't his first priority. First, he wanted her completely naked, like him.

He moved to the edge of the bed, grabbed her foot and tugged until the chunky-heeled, alligator-skin boot came free. He did the same to the other, then took his time sneaking his fingers up the hem of her jeans so he could roll off the lacy socks she wore underneath.

She helped the process by releasing the buttons of her jeans and then lifting her hips so he could divest her of her denim. Now, the only barrier to him enjoying a full and complete view of her lusciously nude body were her panties, and that wasn't much of a barrier for a man like him.

He kissed a path from her ankle to her knee. Like her shoulders and arms, her skin was smooth and tanned. Living on the Texas coast, she probably spent hours in the sun; her flesh graduated in color from the spiced caramel of her toes to the creamy ivory of her inner thighs.

"Oh, James," she cooed as he spread her knees wide enough for him to look his fill while he marked her with one, strong suck on the sensitive skin.

He used a single finger to part her tight curls, drawing a lazy path through the pink, pulsing folds of her sex. Inhaling the intoxicating scent of her need, he felt his cock twitch and tighten. Oh, yeah, it was going to be inside there real soon—but not before he'd blazed the path first with his tongue.

He took an exploratory taste.

"Allie, honey," he growled. "You taste so sweet."

She dragged her hands into his hair, her fingernails scraping at his scalp. She managed to mutter his name, but not much else. And that was just fine with him. He didn't want talking now. He wanted tasting and pleasuring and the utter and complete freedom of knowing that for this moment in time, Allie Barrie belonged to him and only him.

ALLIE COULDN'T FORM a sentence, couldn't hold tight to a single coherent thought. Her awareness was completely and utterly focused on the feel of James's hands, lips, teeth and tongue. She had no idea how long he'd been feasting on her, but he was taking his time just like he always did, milking every ounce of sensation out of her, coaxing her with patient, precise pleasures until every inch of her skin was on fire with need.

But Allie wasn't like a firework. She never had been. She didn't flare up and explode. She was a slow burn that took stoking attention—the kind that a man like Hook knew how to give.

He carved his tongue through the grooves and crevices of her sex, ignoring her clit until it was thick and swollen and needful. He used his fingers to open her up, then concentrated his loving on the part of her that needed him most.

But he didn't forget the rest. He laid aside his feast from time to time to make love to her belly button with his tongue, bite and suck her nipples, then her throat until she was sure she had red, swollen marks all over her skin. But she didn't care—the sensations were worth the price of branding.

When he covered her mouth with his, she could taste her own flavors on his lips for an instant before she was overwhelmed by the unique spices that were his and his alone.

"You still take a while to come, don't you?" he asked, slipping a finger inside her.

Even as her snug flesh wrapped around him, she couldn't deny the truth. "Thankfully, you were always patient."

"Man like me appreciates a challenge. Oh, you feel that?" he said, pressing a second finger inside her, "You're so tight. How long has it been since…?"

"What?"

She was having trouble concentrating on the conversation while he was stroking her so rhythmically, so deeply.

"How long since your last lover?"

She shook her head, not just because thinking about another man was the last thing she wanted to do, but because the memory was too distant to grab on to easily. "A long time."

"Why? Aren't there any hot guys in swimsuits parading up and down the beach?"

He found her clit with his thumb and toggled with

just enough pressure to make her gasp. "Hot guys are a dime a dozen. I want—I want, oh—"

"You want to come," he supplied.

"Yes."

He pressed deeper, fuller. "You're going to, honey. You're going to come so long and loud that my dogs are going to come running. I'm just not sure when. There's a lot yet to do. A lot yet to see."

He was teasing her. Taunting her. She had a moment of clarity enough to realize that he was enjoying this, both in a good way and bad. Of all the men she'd ever been with, none had possessed the power over her that Hook had. He'd never used that power against her.

Not until now.

"Look at all you want. Taste and touch and torture all you want," she said. "Just don't get out of this bed before I've screamed your name."

He grinned. "What about me screaming your name?"

Allie's insides melted, and from the way he increased the pressure of his touch, she knew he felt her intensified need. He had all the power, but he didn't mind sharing. When she pushed him onto his back, he didn't let her go, didn't stop stroking her, so she spent a full minute riding his hand until tiny pops of pleasure nearly left her blind.

"You'd...better..."

"Stop?" he asked.

"Unless you're ready to go the distance."

He shook his head, his dark hair shining blue in the bright light against the stark white pillow. He released her, giving her a second to regain her equilibrium while he folded his hands behind his head and took on the expression she imagined would look at home on a cat who'd just eaten a canary.

She tried to scowl at him, but she was sure with her hair all mussed and her skin flushed pink with pleasure, she didn't look very threatening.

"You're a piece of work, James Hooker."

"A fine piece of work," he agreed. "One that you haven't seen in a good long while, so look your fill."

She bit the inside of her mouth to keep herself from laughing. He'd always been confident with his body, but she supposed he had every reason to be. He'd been riding rodeo since before he was in the double digits, so he'd grown up lean but muscled. And being off the circuit for nearly a decade hadn't made him softer, though he was more filled out in all the right places. She stretched her hands down his sides and then across his pecs, hard with muscle but soft with hair. She bent forward and kissed a path from the center of his throat to the middle of his chest. She diverged long enough to slip her tongue around his nipples, tugging tight in the way she loved when he did it to her.

His pleasured groan told her she'd hit the mark.

She moved lower, spanning her hands over his stomach, her thumbs tracing down the outline of his pelvis. Then her mouth trailed downward until her chin met the hot tip of his erection.

His sharp intake of breath told her what he wanted.

Not that she needed to be told. She'd wanted to take him into her mouth from the first moment he'd thrown off his boxers.

And since she finally had him where she wanted him, she did.

Cradling his balls in her palm, she stroked the full length of him, slipping her tongue over his tip until he rustled beneath her. She tossed her hair back, remembering how much he loved to watch her. When he started murmuring her name, extolling her beauty and cursing the universe for making him wait this long to have her again, she took him fully into her mouth.

The sensations fired her nearly as much as they fired him. He was salty and hard like a savory treat laced with an intoxicating blend of flavors concocted just to drive a woman wild. She loved everything about this—everything about him. She loved how her mouth was full of his heat, how her jaw ached and her lungs burned for air.

Then before she knew it, he'd torn her away and positioned her beneath him, the swollen head of his cock pressed just hard enough against her to reawaken her body, but not enough to join them together.

"You make me crazy," he said, his eyes wild with need.

She desperately wanted to wrap her legs around his waist and force him inside, but they needed protection. She was on birth control, but no matter what foolishness she'd blurted out earlier, now wasn't the time to be stupid, no matter how delicious stupid might prove to be.

"Condom!" she cried.

"Shit," he said, rolling over and tearing open the drawer behind his bed with such force, the contents flew onto the floor.

He managed to snag a square packet from what was left, tear it open and sheath his erection in record time. And then he was inside her.

But not all the way. Oh, no. That would be too easy. Too satisfying. Too instantaneously explosive and satisfying.

He was going to draw this out—because he knew that drawing it out was the only way to reach the end.

"Oh, baby," he said, pressing an inch or two farther inside. "Yeah, you're so tight, but wet. Feel me?"

She wrapped her legs around him. "Please. More."

He gave her another inch, withdrew, then pressed in beyond the snugness.

She gasped for breath. "More."

He struck hard and because the pain was utter bliss, she wanted him to do it again.

"Again."

He slammed into her a second time, holding himself hard inside her until she could gather enough breath to beg him one more time.

"Again. Harder. James. Do it, James. Don't stop. I want you. Don't stop."

He listened. Heaven help her, but he granted her wishes, over and over and over, until she teetered on the brink of release, her entire body engaged in the single act of achieving orgasm, of finding that brief and momentary euphoria that came only from the wild and raw joining of man to woman. She was vaguely aware of him suckling her neck, nipping at her breasts, cradling her ass with his hands while he moved her into the precise position for full penetration—but it wasn't until he pressed his thumb to her center that she finally screamed out as she'd promised and tumbled over the edge, taking him with her every step of the way.

5

JUST BEFORE DAWN, James eased away from Allie's intoxicating warmth and tried not to wince out loud when his bare feet hit the cold floor. She stirred for a second, her soft moan acting like a siren's call. His body wanted nothing more than to climb back into bed with her and stay there until the sun stirred her awake so they could share a round of morning sex.

But his body had been in charge for most of the evening and the whole of the night. It was time for his brain to kick in, and for that he needed caffeine and a few minutes out of Allie's snare. He needed to brew coffee, feed the dogs and prepare for the visit from his investors that was scheduled for noon.

He threw on a fresh pair of jeans and a T-shirt, then padded into the hallway and shut the door behind him. He didn't need light to get to the kitchen, so he didn't squint against the glare until he opened up the fridge to pull out the cream. Whining and scratching at the back door told him the dogs had finally come back from the rabbit hunt or possum run that had kept them occupied last night. After setting the coffeemaker to Brew, he quietly unlatched the back door and immediately gave them an order to stay quiet while he let them in to eat.

His dogs weren't the most obedient gang of mutts he'd ever had, but they listened well enough when they wanted food. Blue, a yellow lab pup now just a year old, danced around like a rodeo clown while Lieba, the German shepherd, strode into the kitchen and sat beside her dish, waiting to be served. Buggabear, an ornery chow-lab mix with a tricky disposition, remained laid out on the porch, his paws hanging coolly over the side, as if James's opening of the door didn't mean a thing to him one way or another.

He'd eat when he was hungry and not before—and this was, as always, just fine with everyone.

Leaving the back door ajar for when Bugga decided he was hungry, James scooped portions of kibble into the three dishes he kept beside the pantry and then poured himself a cup of joe. Liking the drink best when it was hot enough to burn his tongue, he took a long draft and closed his eyes, waiting while the chemicals worked their magic on his bloodstream. He'd worked many long days since deciding to turn the J. Roger into a rodeo destination, but he'd rarely woken up quite this exhausted. Apparently, sex worked different muscles than any he used on the ranch.

Not that he was complaining.

A measured growl drew his attention away from the window, where he'd been sightlessly watching the sky turn from inky black to navy.

"You might want to stand still a minute," he suggested at the sight of Allie in the doorway.

Not that Allie looked like she was moving. Wrapped in nothing but his patchwork quilt, she stood frozen just a few feet from where Lieba was looking up from her bowl, baring her teeth.

When Blue noticed, however, the tension broke. The lab pup let out a yippy bark and bounded over to the newcomer with so much enthusiasm, his paws slipped on the linoleum before he caught his footing. He leaped up, causing Allie to squeal and twist until the quilt surrounded her like a candy wrapper.

And dammit if James didn't have an insatiable sweet tooth.

"Blue, down," James commanded, casting a glance over to Lieba, who'd gone back to her breakfast.

The dog obeyed, but only because James grabbed him by his collar and popped him on the nose. "He loves new people. He also loves old people, cats, squirrels, possums and butterflies."

With a wiggle that awakened a part of his anatomy James had thought he had under control, Allie loosened the quilt enough so that she could bend down and give Blue a pat. Of course, the dog preferred to lick her face and since he'd just been eating his kibble, Allie's expression turned from delighted to grossed-out in about three seconds flat.

"Blue!"

"It's okay," she said, wiping the slobber with a corner of his blanket. "I like animals. I work with them every day."

"Aren't yours usually of the cold-blooded variety?"

"No, actually. I specialize in dolphins. They're mammals. Warm-blooded."

"But no fur," he noted.

She laughed. "No, no fur. But we keep a bunch of dogs at the facility. None that are mine, exactly, but we all look out for them. So this is Blue?"

The dog allowed her to scratch him behind the ears before he finally lost interest and trotted back to his dish.

"And the mean one?"

"Lieba? She's not the mean one. She just looks it because she's a shepherd. She's an ex-police dog. Pop got her from a nearby jurisdiction to help with a man-hunt a couple of years ago, and when her handler ran off with a bronco rider from Banyon Creek, she stayed. She's real sweet when you're not interrupting the most important meal of the day."

Allie shuffled over to the sink, picked up his abandoned coffee cup and took a sip, wincing when she realized he hadn't added any sugar. "Then which one's the mean one?"

James whistled, hoping for once that the ornery pack leader on the porch would heed his call. It was hit or miss, as Bugga had belonged to his uncle and hadn't exactly decided if his loyalty would transfer to his heir.

Surprisingly, the chow cross ambled into the kitchen. His golden eyes lit instantly on Allie and the thick black mane surrounding his massive neck bristled and thickened. James took a step forward and held out his hand. The dog didn't growl—but he never did. Warnings weren't his style.

Allie set down the cup. "Good Lord. I thought the shepherd was huge."

"He's one hundred pounds of trouble," James said. "But he generally likes women."

"I thought you said you never invite women here," she countered.

"Not for overnight stays," he clarified, though he hadn't brought any dates here, even for short visits. But he'd had cowgirls who'd trained here, too, and Bugga generally had a preference for those of the so-called weaker sex.

James took a knee, then grabbed Allie's hand and tugged her down. She nearly tripped all wrapped up, but managed to lower herself.

"I thought you're supposed to show dogs that you're the boss," she said.

"No one bosses Buggabear but Buggabear. You're better off just showing him that you aren't a threat. Once you're a friend, you're a friend for life. Trust me. I once had to pull a chicken bone out of the back of his throat with my one good hand."

"And he didn't bite it off?"

"Gave me a slobber facial as soon as it was free and then slept on my floor for a week."

She swallowed thickly, but extended her hand to the dog all the same. He slunk over, sniffed, eyed her warily, then bent his head forward so she could pet him properly. When his tail started to wag, James relaxed, stood and grabbed another mug so she could sweeten her coffee the way she liked.

"Any others in this pack that I need to meet?" she asked, standing.

Bugga headed over to the food bowls. Blue and Lieba had already finished their meals. Lieba was lying underneath the kitchen table licking her paws while Blue had grabbed a dish towel off the counter and was battling it for supremacy.

"These three run the J. Roger, though they occasionally bring friends home." He handed her the sugar bowl and a spoon, topped off his coffee and then wandered out onto the porch. She joined him a minute later, Blue dancing around her for an instant before he tore off into the yard to chase what James suspected was one of the cats.

The sky had now turned violet. The animals on the property started to stir and he stretched, knowing he had a busy morning ahead of him. On any other day, he'd have had his boots on by now and would be shoveling hay into the horse stalls, but standing here in the silence with Allie felt nice. Especially since he knew that she wasn't wearing a stitch of clothing underneath that quilt.

"Last night was amazing," she murmured, sipping from her mug.

He set his coffee down and surrendered to the impulse to tug her close. "Yeah, it was. Sex was never an issue between us."

"Nothing was ever an issue between us. Not until the baby. Not until you hurt your hand because of me."

James tugged her forward and placed a kiss on the crown of her head. "I don't know how often I can say this, Allie. That wasn't your fault."

"Feels like it was."

"We both made mistakes," he said. "I don't blame you anymore. Haven't for a while."

"Then why did it take so long for me to get back in your bed again?"

She snuggled against him and unable to help himself, he snaked his hand into the wraparound quilt and pulled her closer. Her hair still smelled like peaches, but her skin sizzled with the lingering scents of cooled sweat and hot sex. His jeans tightened around his crotch as his body responded. The horses could wait a little while, couldn't they?

But by the time he tended to the animals, the crew working on the arena would have arrived, along with the women from the diner—including Allie's Aunt May-lene, who'd be catering the event. His initial plan was for Allie to have left, but now, he wasn't so anxious to let her go.

"We hurt each other bad. I didn't want to open my-self to that kind of pain again. I've sort of had my fill."

Beneath the blanket, she locked her hand with his. "Yeah, you have. But that was physical. You've been recovered for a long time."

"Wasn't just my hand that hurt," he confessed. "The whole thing messed me up. Losing use of my hand, my career, my girl…my baby."

She eased away from him and pulled the blanket tighter. "She was *our* baby."

"She?" His heart seized. He hadn't been privy to the details of Allie's miscarriage. He'd still been in the hospital, enduring one of four surgeries he'd had to try and repair the damage to his hand. He hadn't found out about her losing the baby until weeks after it had hap-pened, when he'd been in rehab. And he hadn't even found out from her. His father had broken the news when he'd asked why Allie hadn't come around for so long.

Truth be told, the loss had nearly broken his heart in two. He'd been nineteen and terrified that he didn't have it in him to be a decent father to anyone, but that hadn't mattered when he'd learned that he wasn't even going to get the chance.

"I don't really know what the baby was," she said. "I was only about five weeks along when I lost her. Or him. I just think of her as a girl, I guess."

"*When* you think of her."

The comment came out hard and the snap sparked a flash of anger in her eyes. "Of course I think of her."

"You moved on pretty damned fast," he countered.

"How the hell would you know what I went through? You were dealing with your own troubles. I wasn't going to add mine on top of them. That's why I left. I asked you if you wanted me to stay, but you said I should worry about myself. I wrote to you. Emails. Letters. I called every week. You're the one who stopped answering the phone."

He remembered, but only vaguely. He wanted to blame the painkillers and leftover anesthetics, but the truth was, he hadn't wanted to deal. His brain had been on overload, first with trying to process how he was going to provide for a child when he'd lost his livelihood and then learning that he not only didn't have a kid to worry about anymore, but the girl he'd hoped would share his life had decided to go off to the coast to lick her own wounds. After a couple of weeks of being on his own, he'd decided they were both better off apart.

Seemed like a really selfish choice in the light of this new day.

"You're right, I was."

From the stables, he heard a series of whinnies that were only going to get louder as the sun rose in the eastern sky. He had a boatload of work to do and as much as he might understand how working things out with Allie should be a priority, he also knew it would have to wait.

"We still have a lot to talk about," she said, her voice so sad, he was surprised to see her eyes were dry.

"Yeah, I think we do. But I have to—"

She waved off his excuse before he made it. "I understand. You have a lot going on today. I'll just get dressed and get out of here. Maybe we can hook up later."

She turned to go, but James snagged a corner of the blanket and pulled her back. "Don't go. I mean, you don't have to leave, though I think getting off the porch might be a good idea because the crew ought to be here any minute. Take a shower. If you're up to it, whip us up some breakfast. I won't have much time to eat, but I did promise to show you the arena, right? You can stick around, maybe, and then we'll finish this tonight?"

"Finish?"

"Our talk," he clarified. Just yesterday, he would have been certain that one roll in the sack with Allie would have been enough to put the last vestiges of their long-ago love to rest, but now he wasn't so sure.

Not sure at all.

She nodded and the tiny smile that lit her face rivaled the morning sun. "I do make a terrific omelet."

"Dazzle me," he encouraged.

She rolled her eyes. "What do you think I've been trying to do?"

He kissed her on the cheek, then spun her toward the door and patted her on the ass so she got inside before the trucks he heard rumbling up the gravel drive came around back and caught her in nothing but a bedspread.

"Drive me crazy," he answered. "And you're succeeding."

She turned and stuck her tongue out at him before she went back into the kitchen. He grinned and whistled for the dogs to come out, shutting the door behind her just as she crossed into the hallway and disappeared on the way back to his room. He dropped onto the porch step, tugged on the boots he kept on the stoop and then grabbed one of the dusty hats off the pegs and started toward the barn.

Never in a million years had he imagined he'd let

Allie Barrie into his life again, but he had. He wasn't entirely certain he'd been joshing when he said he'd lost his mind, but he figured by the day's end, he'd find out.

6

ALLIE HEARD THE TRUCKS as she ambled lazily toward James's room. Since she had no idea who was there or how likely they were to come inside the house without knocking, she scurried inside his bedroom and locked the door behind her, listening for the sound of anyone strolling inside. But all she heard were the dogs barking and then shouts of greeting from men who had clearly been up for more than an hour, judging by the energy in their voices. When they came around the side of the house, she heard their dialogue through the windows, which were opened to the breeze, though the blinds were down.

"Whose car is that out front, Hook? Looks a bit like Allie Barrie's coupe. Don't tell me she finally tracked you down and got you in her clutches."

Allie frowned. She didn't recognize the voice, but she was pretty sure she wanted to punch the face of whomever it belonged to.

"Never you mind who my houseguests are, Starkey. I've got the horses handled. Take the crew to the arena and get to work on that ramp for the handicapped sec-tion. And make sure the kid from the satellite company has the feed to the production room set up. Seen Maylene yet?"

Starkey, whom Allie knew was James's old buddy from high school, mumbled something about James messing with fire before he replied, "She's still at the diner. Sent us out with fresh doughnuts and said she was doing her prep work and seeing to her customers at the restaurant, but that she'd be out here to set up by ten."

"That'll do," James answered. "I've got about an hour's worth of work around here and then I'll meet you up at the site. If you need anything, use the cell phone."

An hour? That wasn't a lot of time…but it would be enough if she got serious about making the most of it. With his investors heading to the ranch today to check on the progress of the arena, real life was intruding on the sensual fantasy they'd started last night in his bed. But that didn't mean she couldn't make the most of the little time they had left—if she stopped listening at windows. She dropped the blanket, snagged her overnight bag and headed into the bathroom for a shower.

She was just toweling off when she heard a knock on the bedroom door. Wrapping the terry cloth around her, she padded across the room and whispered, "Hook?"

"Yeah, it's me."

She unlocked the door. "I wasn't sure who comes and goes through here."

"Good precaution," he said, closing the door behind her. "No one generally comes inside without an invitation, but you can't be too careful when you're butt-naked."

"I'm not naked anymore," she said.

With one determined tug of her towel, he rectified the situation, then dropped to his knees and pulled her forward so that his mouth made immediate contact with her bare stomach. Her nipples tightened into electric pinpoints of heat.

"Now, you're naked. And warm and clean and wet. Just how I like my women."

Allie laughed, even as his kisses sent a lightning storm of thrills through her body. "Stop!" She pushed at his shoulders, though not with much conviction. "Don't you have horses to take care of?"

"They're all fat and underworked," he lied. "They can wait fifteen minutes for their breakfast."

"Fifteen minutes isn't long enough for what you want," she claimed.

"You think?" he asked, running his callused hands over her bare bottom as he dipped his head lower. "I bet I can make you come in fifteen minutes. Time me."

The feel of his tongue parting her sex nearly sent her into a tizzy. She was sore down there from all the loving she'd had last night, but the soothing mix of his moist flesh and the fresh water from the shower made her want to work through the discomfort.

"You know I'm not that easy."

She dug her hands into his hair and obeyed without thought when he ran his hand down her leg and then guided it over his shoulder.

"Never easy," he murmured into her skin. "But worth the effort."

The pleasure spiking through her pricked at her heart. Allie had never been one of those women who could will herself to an orgasm. In fact, all the feminist cries that she was responsible for her own pleasure had chipped at her confidence for the years following her breakup with James. In all the lovers she'd had since him—and admittedly, there hadn't been many—none had accepted the challenge of helping her achieve climax with the verve that Hook always had. He'd always considered it his solemn responsibility to make sure she came long, hard and often.

And clearly, he hadn't changed.

When her knees started to buckle from spasms of pleasure, he pushed her onto the bed, positioning her so that her bottom was barely on the edge. He spread her legs wide and slurped, suckled, bit and tugged at her labia and clit until the room started to spin. By the time he dropped his pants and slipped on a condom, she was close to the edge, simmering with the kind of heat that could explode with the slightest provocation.

Luckily, there was nothing slight about James. He grabbed her hands and pulled her into a sitting position before he knelt down in front of her and pushed inside.

The sensation of the position shattered her equilibrium. She clutched at his shoulders even while she flattened her feet on the ground.

"Yeah," he encouraged, smoothing his hands down her thighs. "Got yourself some leverage there, now. Here, let's add this."

He grabbed a pillow and positioned it just under her bottom to angle her. When he thrust forward, her entire world went wonky.

"Oh!" she cried.

"Yeah, sweetheart. That's it. Meet me halfway and I'll take you over the top."

The position was intimate—his mouth to her mouth, then lower to her breasts, then back up to her face. She released him, bracing her arms behind her so that arching her back completed the last adjustment. His strong, purposeful thrusts hit her in the precise spot that flared her climax. By the time he stood, pushed her back and pounded so hard into her she thought she'd ascended into sensation heaven, her climax burst open the last of her inhibitions and she was screaming out nonsensical words of amazement without giving a damn that the windows were open and the whole ranch could hear.

He rolled over beside her. With his jeans dangling around his ankles, he looked like the schoolboy she'd fallen so deeply in love with. His chest heaved and when their eyes met, they both dissolved into laughter.

"Told you," he said, turning his wrist so she could see his watch.

She hadn't marked the time, but she had no doubt that he'd accomplished his goal within the deadline. James Hooker never made a promise he couldn't keep—never.

"I want to do that again," she confessed.

"Honey, so do I, but even I have my limits."

She rolled over onto her side and slapped him lightly on the chest. "Not now! Later. After you're done impressing your investors. Of course, the whole of the J. Roger probably heard what just happened. If I was them, I'd be impressed."

He chuckled. "The arena's clear on the other side of the property. You can scream all you want and no one's gonna hear you but me. And I do love that sound. And I'm going to hear it again. And again. And again. As soon as all these strangers are off my land."

He kissed her softly, in utter contrast to the sex they'd just shared, which had been hot and hard and explosive. As he did so, he kicked off his boots and pants, then allowed her to pull his T-shirt over his head and bathe his chest in wet kisses before he climbed off the bed and headed toward the bathroom for a shower.

She grabbed the pillow he'd placed underneath her and tugged it against her chest, unable to stop the wash of disappointment that scudded through her. Though she'd had more sex in the last twelve hours than she'd had in the previous twelve months, she wanted more. More sex. More orgasms. More Hook.

Much, much more.

But how much more could she handle? At some point, she was going to have to make a decision about where this was going. Her first goal, to work her way back into his bed, had been achieved. Now she had to see if it was viable for her to remain in his life for longer than a couple of nights.

And this time around, it wasn't just up to him. To make a reunion work, she was going to have to change the direction of her own future—a decision she'd thought she'd been ready to make.

But was she?

JAMES GRABBED A FADED red bandanna from the bed of his truck and wiped the sweat from his face. He glanced up at the sky, and, figuring the hour to be just shy of noon, he decided he didn't have time for another shower before the investors showed. He tore off his perspiration-ripe shirt, grabbed a bottled water and poured half of it into the fabric and gave himself a working-man's bath.

On any other day, he might have been able to return to the house and clean up in less than ten minutes, but now that Allie was there, he knew he'd take much, much longer. Just as his uncle had warned, the woman was one-hundred-percent distraction. A beautiful, sensual, mind-blowing distraction—one he hadn't been expecting, wasn't prepared for and sure as hell didn't know how to resist.

But he had to find a way—at least for the long-term. She looked damned luscious in his house and felt perfectly at home in his kitchen, his bed, his life. Yet despite all their teenage dreams, he knew better than to think this fantasy was going to last more than a couple of days. Allie had to finish her doctorate—and beyond that, she had the job offer. He had no doubt that wherever she ended up, it would be somewhere with a lot more to offer her than the J. Roger ever could.

"Hope you remembered to pack something clean to wear before those big shots show up," Maylene Drummond said, her hands wringing through the folds of her apron as she walked up from the barbecue area. "Unless they're women, in which case I highly suggest you remain shirtless."

James spun around in time to catch Allie's aunt give him a saucy wink.

He smiled and tugged a clean button-down out of the bag in the back of his truck. "I'm not a hillbilly, Miss Maylene. I do know how to clean up for company."

"You clean up for my niece, too? 'Cause don't think I didn't see her car parked out in front of your house on my way out here."

"I would never assume you wouldn't notice such an important detail."

She scowled and for an instant, James was sorry he'd added a tinge of sass to his reply. Miss Maylene was a Lost Gun institution in the making, as she wasn't quite old enough to achieve that small-town status just yet. In her late forties, she was as petite as her niece, but infinitely more compact. He'd seen her physically remove inebriated roustabouts from her diner for cursing—and not even break a sweat. He knew he was safe when the left side of her mouth tilted into a half grin, as if she found the whole situation with him and Allie amusing, despite the repercussions they both knew could bring a whole lot of people more pain than they deserved.

"I'm no gossip, James Hooker. And I'm not a busy-body, neither. I gave that sweet girl the apartment over my diner so she didn't have her every coming and going examined by her father or his new wife."

New being a relative term. Allie's father had remarried nearly six years ago. But it said a lot that his sister still considered the spouse to be an interloper.

"I'm sure Allie appreciates the privacy, but your place is pretty crowded, too. We figured coming out to the J. Roger was a better idea. You have to give us points for not taking this to town," he said.

She harrumphed. "Whatever *this* is, I suppose?"

He shrugged. He couldn't tell her what *this* was. He didn't really know—and wasn't sure he'd say even if he did. He and Allie had enjoyed a spectacular night and even more invigorating morning. He could get used to having a woman like her around permanently, even though he knew the chances of that happening were between zero and none.

"Allie and I have a lot to…work out."

"Is that what you kids are calling it now?" she asked saucily, then waved her hand as if she really didn't want an answer. "I'll play along. I'd rather you two settle your business out here anyway. I open early and my predawn regulars would have had a mighty fine time spreading the news of your walk of shame all over Lost Gun."

"I have nothing to be ashamed of," he countered while he thrust his arms into the sleeves of his shirt and attempted to fasten up the front as best he could. The fingers of his right hand were showing the signs of all the hard work he'd been putting into the arena in the past few weeks. Stiff and throbbing, they had a hard time working the buttons.

He was only glad none of the guys were around to

see Miss Maylene slap his hands aside so she could do the job herself.

"No, you don't. You could do a lot worse than my niece."

"Trouble is, she could do a lot better than me."

"How the hell do you figure that? You're a fine specimen of a man and you know it. I don't recall you ever having trouble catching the interest of the young girls in town."

"I'm not trying to be humble, Miss Maylene. I'm not a bad catch for a woman who'd be happy living out in the middle of nowhere. But let's be honest. Allie's got bigger ambitions."

"How would you know?"

"She spent a heck of a lot of her daddy's money paying for her education. I'm not sure what someone with a doctorate in marine biology is going to do in landlocked Lost Gun, do you?"

Maylene frowned. The woman was a paragon of common sense and it didn't take a whole lot to see that what he was saying was true. By building this arena on the land he'd inherited from his uncle, James had ensured that the rest of his life was going to be spent on the J. Roger Ranch. Unless, of course, the whole venture failed.

But even if it did, he still couldn't imagine himself living anywhere but here. Lost Gun was in his blood.

After giving his collar a tug for good measure, she gave his cheek two gentle pats, then one stinging slap, clearly to get his attention.

"You let Allie decide what she wants to do with her life and her education. The only way she can do that is if she finally comes to term with whatever is left—or isn't—between you. She's been chasing after you for an awful long time, Hook. You just play it fair with her and things'll work out however they're meant to."

He nodded in agreement. He didn't want to play games with Allie, and while he certainly didn't want to mislead her in any way, he wasn't about to push her away now because of his concerns over her future. She had to make the choices she had to make—and he had to make his.

"Right now, the only thing I'm worried about working out is impressing my investors with our progress. I hope you trotted out your best barbecue."

She rolled her eyes. "Honey, I don't serve anything that isn't my best. And Allie even gave me some advice when she first got here about how to talk up the—what was it she said?—*sustainability* of my food. Says it'll appeal to their bottom line that my menu is local and that I grow my own herbs and grind my own spices. Something about foodies, whatever the hell they are."

James chuckled. He had no idea what Allie had been talking about, but if it sounded good to the investors, he was all for it. "You just make sure they know how much money they're going to make off of concessions. That's all they'll care about. That and the flavor of the food. Nothing makes a man happier than a stomach full of delicious food."

Maylene rolled her eyes. "That ain't true, James Hooker, but as you're not converting the J. Roger into a chicken ranch, delicious food will have to do."

7

By THE TIME A TRIO of double-cab trucks came up the drive, James was ready for them. He greeted his cousin first and then shook hands with the representatives from the bank, the rodeo association board and an aide from the office of his state congressman. Home-grown businesses were a high priority in this part of the country. The J. Roger would generate more than just attention for Lost Gun, which had turned out more rodeo stars per capita than any other town in Texas.

By the time he'd finished the tour and led the group over to the umbrella-topped picnic tables for lunch, he'd relaxed and concentrated on enjoying his accomplishments. His construction crew's progress had been just short of miraculous. The training facility would be a top-notch draw for the best of the best, and the arena, with its booming sound system, high-tech flat screens and comfortable seating, would take the rodeo experience up to levels not unlike a big-draw concert, which was what they planned to use the place for when the rodeo wasn't in town.

These men had sunk a ton of cash into the project and judging by the infectious grins and back-patting, the afternoon had been a success. And when he caught sight of Allie helping her aunt portion out her famous brisket onto plates lined with cheery red-checked paper, he knew he hadn't had a better day in a hell of a long time.

"Here you go."

When she swapped places with Maylene so she could deliver food to the table and reached across to set a plate in front of him, his stomach wasn't the only part of his anatomy growling with hunger.

"Thanks, sweetheart," he whispered. "This is the kind of service I could get used to."

Her green eyes widened. "Could you really?"

But before he could form a response, his cousin butted in to the conversation.

"Allie? Allie Barrie, what the heck are you doing back in Lost Gun serving barbecue? You didn't have a nasty run-in with a shark that sent you scrambling back to dry land, did you?"

Paul, who'd graduated a year ahead of Allie and one year behind James, stood up with an opened arm, which Allie fell into for a friendly hug.

"Sharks get a bad rap," she countered. "I'm just helping my aunt out today, what with so many important people coming out to the J. Roger."

Each and every one of the men blushed and grinned like fools. Allie certainly did have that effect on people—even him.

Especially him.

"I hope all you gentleman know that this is the best food this part of Texas has to offer," James added.

"Your wives' and your mamas' home-cooking excepted, of course," Allie tossed in.

The investors laughed, and, as some had already dug

into the moist and crusty meat, they yummed and nodded in agreement.

Paul took his seat, but didn't let Allie leave. "I thought you were in the Caribbean working for that new resort that's building a billion-dollar aquarium."

Allie threw James a quick glance as she put a couple of baskets of jalapeño corn bread in the center of the table. They hadn't had a chance to talk much about her job offer. He had no idea it would take her as far away as the Caribbean islands.

"My doctorate advisor has been the main consultant on the project since its inception. He's offered me a position supervising the mammalian habitats, but I haven't decided what I'm going to do yet."

James concentrated on busting up the brisket with his fork, which wasn't hard since the meat was tender as silk. He took a bite and tried to let the burst of beefy flavor distract him. He could feel Allie's gaze on him, but he resisted every urge to react. He had no business influencing her decision one way or another.

"Have you been down there? I hear it's spectacular," Paul gushed. "I went to a time-share presentation about a year ago up in Dallas and I gotta tell you, if not for the state of the economy, I might have signed up on the spot. Hell, if this arena draws in the big names like we think it will, I just might!"

Beside him, the congressman's aide started peppering him with questions about projections for the economic impact on this part of Texas, but James had a hard time concentrating when the visual of Allie in a bikini, lounging on a white-sand beach with an umbrella drink, popped into his brain. He took a sip of sweet tea and pushed the image away. Scientists like Allie didn't sunbathe. At least, he didn't think they did. Who would relax in the sun and surf when you had to work in it every day? Or was Allie the type of researcher who was kept holed up in a laboratory so that the lure of paradise might be enough to make her take the first cruise ship out of Houston?

"I've been out there twice, but there wasn't much to see. Most of the work Dr. Rayburn oversees involves the integration of the local sea life into the design of the resort. It's amazing, actually. The incorporation of natural ocean habitats into the vacation experience is beyond anything I've ever heard of. It's like eco-tourism on steroids. It's very exciting."

James frowned. For some reason, hearing her speak with such ease and expertise made him lose his appetite.

"You must be chomping at the bit to be a part of it," Paul continued.

This time, when she threw James a sidelong glance, she caught him staring. "I'm not sure what I want to do just yet. I've spent so much time in school, it's hard to conceptualize the future as a real and tangible thing. Especially a future so far away from home."

James nodded and force-fed himself another bite of meat. No doubt, the congressman's aide thought he was agreeing with his assessment that the addition of a cell tower and the near completion of the impressive satellite hub would do wonders for bringing J. Roger events to an international audience via livestreaming. But he could hardly make sense of the man's chatter. Allie was on the brink of making serious, life-changing decisions. She'd come home to find her direction and he was only now beginning to understand the weight of it all.

When he'd first invited her to follow him home last night, he'd figured that they had some talking to do— some real conversing that would put the past behind them for good. But it had turned into a hot and steamy reunion between two people who'd been sexually compatible since their first fumbling romp in the back of his flatbed truck. Waking up with her this morning had been like opening his eyes in heaven.

But how long could it last when she had so much more she needed to do with her life?

He'd promised Maylene that he wouldn't make decisions for Allie about her future and he meant to keep that vow. But that didn't mean he wasn't going to encourage her to make her choice once and for all—and sooner rather than later.

AFTER THE BIGWIGS CLIMBED back into their trucks, full to the brim with Maylene's awesome cooking and pleased as punch with the progress of the J. Roger Arena, Allie accepted James's invitation to see the place on a private tour. They strolled alone through the cavernous main building, her left hand softly wrapped around his injured right one while he pointed out the modern twists they'd added to the design which elevated the J. Roger above an ordinary rodeo facility.

"So there'll be more than just rodeos here," she said.

"The income has to be steadier than a once- or twice-a-month event. Training will be a huge draw, but an arena this size needs more to make it profitable. We've got three country-music promoters signed up to schedule big events here and several festivals looking at using the land and the arena for weeks at a time in the off-season."

Allie's smile turned into a light chuckle.

"What?" he asked.

"I never thought you'd find your calling as a tycoon."

He matched her laugh. "Hardly. I'm just a guy turning an old man's dream into reality and hoping to make a living at the same time. The J. Roger is a lot of land, but it's not fit for much more than rodeo. Its ranching days are long over and since we're lucky enough to be near a major highway, why not take advantage? Increased tourism will be a shot in the arm for Lost Gun, too. It's win-win."

"Spoken like a real businessman."

He shrugged. "Least my daddy can't say my college tuition didn't get put to good use."

"I always thought he wanted you to follow him into law enforcement. I mean, after you finished riding bulls."

James snorted. "Can you see me and my father working together on a daily basis? The man is single-minded and driven, but he's a little black-and-white for my taste."

"Maybe you have to be in his line of work, especially when you're raising two kids all on your own."

"Speaking of J.R.'s fathering skills," James said, pulling out his cell phone and checking the screen for missed calls. "I haven't heard from Ginny."

Judging by his predictions last night, he'd expected his sister to call him at some point since the big fight at the Gunner place. Allie couldn't help but be pleased that she hadn't.

"That's good, though, right? Means she has things under control and doesn't need her big brother to ride to the rescue?"

He frowned and, from his expression, Allie could tell he wasn't so sure. His relationship with his father had always been complicated and she didn't imagine much had changed.

"Why don't you give her a call if you're worried?"

she suggested. "I can make myself scarce. I really should head back to town at some point."

"Why?"

The question disarmed her. After so many years of chasing him around, she didn't expect he'd be reluctant to let her go, even for just a little while.

"I just thought you might want some space."

He slipped his arm around her waist and pulled her up close. "Now that you're here, I'm finding that I'm not so anxious for you to leave. And that's going to turn out to be damned inconvenient, especially with that big job offer you've got hanging over your head."

"It's not hanging over my head," she denied, opting to ignore the warning she'd gotten from Sam that Eric was anxious for her to make a decision sooner rather than later. The job was a marine biologist's dream. Working in the private sector, the budgets would be huge. She'd have access to sea creatures and scientific equipment that even cutting-edge universities could only dream about.

And then there was the location. A Caribbean island with an annual average temperature of seventy-nine degrees made up for the occasional hurricane threat. It was a hell of lot more enticing than the one-hundred-plus temperatures they sometimes saw in Lost Gun.

But Lost Gun had Hook—and that was no small incentive.

Unfortunately, he was more insightful than she'd given him credit for. He stared at her with one brow arched high, forcing her to revise her claim.

"Okay," she admitted. "It's hanging over my head. Anybody else would have said yes the minute the offer was made. But I haven't. Maybe it was because of the unfinished business between us. Maybe it was something more. It's a big decision and I know it sounds like a no-brainer, but it's not. I have a lot to consider."

They'd wandered to the area just above the chutes, prime seats where the spectators had unhampered views of the cowboys climbing into a nine-by-two-by-six metal cage in order to tempt fate. Allie leaned up against the railing, her hands grasping the bars behind her. James settled into the seat in front of her and kicked his boots up beside her.

"Like?" he asked.

She wasn't going to say, *You*. How pathetic would that be? Not taking an amazing career opportunity just because she was still in love with a guy who hadn't given her the time of day for years until this weekend? Besides, the truth was a lot more complicated.

"This is going to sound crazy," she said, "but I'm not sure marine biology is really what I want to do with my life."

His eyes widened. "You'd better not say that too loud. Your daddy paid good money for that education."

She snorted. "He paid for my undergrad work, but I had scholarships, jobs and internships that covered the rest. I'm not a mooch. Not when I wasn't one-hundred-percent sure what I wanted to do. But I'm good at science and I enjoy the research and the animals. Still, there's always been something holding me back from going full-throttle."

"A doctorate isn't full-throttle? Hell, Allie, you finished your undergraduate work in three years when it should have taken you four. You have one graduate degree and you're about to get another. I'd say that's about as full speed ahead as it gets. And I haven't seen your dad in a while, but I bet he's crazy proud of that PhD you're about to earn."

"Yeah," she agreed, "but he's also big on a person loving what they do. I want to love what I do. I like it a lot, that's for sure. But—"

"But, what? Allie, you'd be living on a resort in the Caribbean, playing with dolphins and chasing starfish all day. What's not to love?"

"Could you do it?"

He clucked his tongue. "I'd go crazy in about five minutes, but I'm not a marine biologist."

"Do you even know what a marine biologist does?" she asked.

"I have no idea. I suppose I haven't given you much of a chance to tell me before this weekend, either. And up until now, I've kept you pretty busy doing things other than talking about science."

A rush of heat suffused through her at the memories. She'd spent nearly every quiet moment since he'd headed out to meet with his investors reliving every touch, every kiss, every intimate lick and taste and thrust. She and James might have the odds stacked against them when it came to career paths and ambitions, but in the department of making love, their compatibility could not be denied.

He sat up, leaning forward so that his elbows were on his knees. "So tell me about your latest, greatest discoveries in the world of marine biology."

She kicked at his boot. "Trust me, you don't want to hear about dolphins and starfish."

"Sure I do. Wouldn't be the first time you talked about them. You've always loved critters from the sea."

"No, I haven't," she argued. "I never thought about marine life back in high school. I only paid attention in biology because Mrs. Frasier stopped by the pharmacy for her mother's heart pills and she reported my grades to my father even before she told me."

"Is that how you remember it?"

"Yes," she insisted, though she had to confess that a lot about school was a blur to her now—except for the parts that had to do with her and James.

"You always had a knack for science," he reminded her. "You helped me out with chemistry at the junior college and you were two years behind me."

She tried to remember and did conjure up an image of poring over college-level textbooks in James's living room and stealing kisses whenever his father wasn't looking.

"Funny how I remember it so differently. I was so messed up when I left Lost Gun, I had no idea what I wanted to do when I got to school. I just fell into marine sciences because my roommate, Samantha, already had her eyes on the program at Port Aransas."

"Well, I can't contradict your memory since I wasn't there," he said, "but as I recall, it was at the state fair your junior year when you refused to ride up to the old barn with me until I won you a stuffed dolphin by playing those rigged games on the fairway."

"Oh, my God," she said, blushing at how she'd once so brazenly bartered sex for a stuffed animal. "I totally forgot about that."

He cursed as if exasperated, though she could tell by the tilt of his grin that he was teasing. "Teddy Bear wouldn't do. Stuffed horse? No way. Had to be that damned fish."

She opened her mouth to correct him, but by the crook of his grin, she knew he'd said *fish* just to get under her skin.

Well, it was working—but not in the way he intended.

Or was it?

It had been years since she'd felt this comfortable teasing and bantering and talking—really talking—to someone she'd just made love with. She hadn't been celibate since they'd broken up, but none of the men she'd dated and certainly not the few that she'd slept with knew her the way James did—and none of them ever would. She and James had been friends since they were kids. Unless she discovered the secret to time travel, no man would ever understand her with the kind of depth as James Hooker.

But did she really want to go backward—or forward?

"I bet my daddy still has that damned 'fish' in his attic. Unless the new Mrs. Barrie threw it out, which is entirely possible."

James stood and gestured so she'd follow him down the stairs to the main ring, which was fluffy with freshly turned-over dirt.

"You don't like your new stepmother?"

She shrugged. "My father's happy and that's all that matters. I don't really know her. She moved to town after I'd gone off to school and I don't see her that often."

"But you would if you lived here again."

Yes, she would. She really hadn't considered that piece of the puzzle. She hadn't had much of a chance to consider anything beyond getting James's attention. Now that she'd done that—and then some—she had some serious thinking to do.

"I guess I would." She kicked a wad of dirt off the step, then eyed James directly. God, he was handsome. His dark hair curled a bit under his cowboy hat and the shadows of the brim did magical things to his sapphire-blue eyes. Her mouth watered at the possibility of them going back to the house and spending the rest of the day and night in bed, but as the air grew thicker with all the complications swirling around her, she decided she needed some time to think.

"Why don't you give your sister a call and I'll go back to the diner? Maybe you can meet me there later for dinner?"

But he immediately shook his head. "I'm not interested in floating our business out for the whole of Lost Gun to weigh in on just yet. Go on if you need to take care of some things, but I'd sure like it if you came back. I can throw a couple of steaks on the grill. Open a bottle of wine."

"You have wine?"

"No," he replied. "But I can get some."

She ran her hand over his cheek, loving the feel of his rough five o'clock shadow against the sensitive skin of her palm. She wanted more than ever to experience that texture on other responsive parts of her body. And she would. Later. After they'd both had time to think.

"Tell you what," she suggested. "You take care of the food and I'll bring the wine."

"Think you can get your hands on one of your aunt's lemon-meringue pies?"

"I'm pretty sure that can be arranged."

He snared her around the waist and when he kissed her, she was immediately struck by the intensity. The crash of his lips on hers, the wild tangle of their tongues, the hard press of his hand—the one the bull had mangled—told her one thing loud and clear. He would let her go, but only after he was certain she was coming back.

8

As he watched Allie's car kick up dirt on its way off the property, James caught sight of another vehicle heading in. He instantly recognized the oversize F-10 truck as the one his father had insisted Ginny drive for safety, despite James's warnings about the trouble teenagers could get into with a flat bed that was so spacious.

Per usual, his father had ignored him. He'd bet his best ranch horse that the old man was regretting it now that Ginny had hooked up with Wade Gunner.

"Was that Allie Barrie I just saw pulling out of here?" Ginny asked after she hopped down from the elevated cab, her hair pulled up in a bouncy ponytail and her eyes, just a tad lighter than a Texas summer sky, free of the redness he would have expected after last night's show.

"Yup."

He didn't add anything else. Now that Allie had left, the significance of the fact that she'd been here at all started to seep in. He'd been weak last night—broken down by his father's humiliating antics over his sister's choice of boyfriends and stressed out over the inspection by the investors. Or maybe he'd been in a nostalgic mood, remembering when he'd been so crazy in love with Allie, he would have been willing to fight off the world in order to be with her.

Whatever the case, the reunion he'd been avoiding had happened and damn if it hadn't been one of the best nights of his life.

The dogs came tearing around from the back, their barks morphing into excited yelps when they recognized who'd shown up this time around. After the parade of strangers they'd endured today, even Buggabear danced in a circle when Ginny attempted to scratch him behind the ears.

Once she had the pack moderately settled, she followed him through the house and into the kitchen, where he pulled out two sodas from the fridge and popped the tops.

"So, are you going to tell me what Allie Barrie was doing here?" she asked.

"Are you going to tell me about you and Wade Gunner?"

"Yes," she sassed.

He should have figured. She hadn't driven all the way out to the ranch to talk about the weather.

"Go ahead, then."

"I asked first."

"Hey, you came out to my place, clearly to unburden your soul. So unburden. I have work to do."

"I can help," she offered.

"Maybe after you tell me whether I need to add 'clean up the spare room' to my to-do list because Pops kicked you out."

"If only," she groused. "He grounded me for lying about where I was last night. I couldn't have left the house at all if I hadn't promised that I was coming here and that I wouldn't make a single stop on the way here or back. And I'd bet a hundred bucks he tracked me on the GPS."

"That's a sucker bet," James said, wiggling his nose as the carbonation from the soda shot up his sinuses. "Of all the kids in that high school of yours, you hook up with the one that's going to get under his craw the most. Was that on purpose?"

"No," she insisted, but James's doubtful stare changed her tune. "Okay, maybe. At first. But not now. Now, I really think I love him."

"But you're not sure?"

"I'm almost eighteen," she said, her tone snapping as if he'd just questioned whether or not water was wet or the sky was blue. "We have fun together. We laugh a lot. We talk a lot. He doesn't rag on Dad, even though he has every reason to. He just says I have to be patient and let Dad get to know him. Then he'll know Wade is more than just a last name or the little brother of the man who gets a kick out of pissing him off. He says if I keep my grades up and don't get in any trouble because of him, Pops'll eventually come around."

James combed a hand through his hair and whistled. "That's mighty grown-up for Pete Gunner's kid brother. Maybe he was adopted?"

His quip drew a reluctant grin out of his sister, the kind of smile that warmed his chest and made him forget, for a moment, about his own volatile love life. Being over a decade older than Ginny, he'd always skirted the line between the roles of protective big brother and surrogate father. Not that J.R. didn't take his job as patriarch seriously, but after losing his wife to hemorrhaging when Ginny was born, he'd become even more overprotective of his children, especially his daughter. She was the last piece he had of his wife and James could understand why J.R. fought so hard against losing her either to cruel fate or, worse, to the family that had been nothing but trouble since they cruised into town.

"I guess someone in that house has to be the grown-up," Ginny conceded. "Though Pete's not so bad, once you get to know him. He's full of the devil, but he stuck up for me last night. Even you didn't do that."

James pulled out a kitchen chair and slid in across from his sister. "You were doing a pretty good job of sticking up for yourself on your own. I figured after that, if you needed me, you'd have called."

"But would you have answered? What with Allie Barrie staying overnight?"

"Who told you she stayed overnight?"

Ginny grinned and sipped her soda. "You just did. Look, I was only a kid when you and Allie were together, but I always liked her. I never understood why she lit out on you after you got hurt."

"She didn't light out. I pushed her out. It was complicated."

"More complicated than me going out with the boy our father would most like to arrest and throw in jail?"

"Believe it or not, yeah."

"Because she was pregnant?"

James felt the air swoosh out of his chest. Ginny hadn't even been in her double-digits when he and Allie's relationship had imploded and since then, the topic of their teenage pregnancy had never been deemed fit for dinner-table discussion. But he and J.R. had fought about the mess on more than one occasion, especially after his father realized that James had pushed Allie away. Ginny must have heard more than either of them intended.

"How do you know about that?"

She took a long sip of her soda, her gaze locked on the grooves on the kitchen table.

"Ginny?"

"I heard Dad and Mr. Barrie talking about it a while back. They talk about it a lot, actually."

James pushed his chair away from the table, but couldn't muster enough strength in his legs to stand. Instead, he just muttered a curse that made his sister's eyebrows pop up high beneath her bangs.

After all these years, he'd never really considered how his and Allie's breakup might have affected the people around them, especially their fathers. As the only two single dads in Lost Gun, Matthew Barrie and J. R. Hooker had become fast friends and confidants. Matt's gentle nature counteracted J.R.'s good-old-boy attitudes, softening J.R. around the edges and opening his mind to alternative parenting strategies to a bootstrap. And Matt's knowledge as a pharmacist had come in handy while J.R., who had stubbornly remained single no matter how many widows and divorcées had flounced around him after his wife's death, dealt with raising a baby who'd been born with colic and suffered from croup and thrush several times before she'd turned three.

James had never understood exactly what J.R. brought to the equation, but even at his most stubborn, the man was loyal to the end. And to most men, that was more than enough to make you a friend for life.

"What do they say?" he asked.

Ginny shifted uncomfortably in her chair as if she realized how hard this topic would be for them to discuss. "Just that it's a shame, how it all went down. How they were sure you two were going to get married and if not for that stupid bull, they'd be sitting on the porch watching their grandchildren tear down the driveway in soap-box cars rather than talking about sports and politics."

James downed his soda. Since he was in the presence of his sister, he belched long and loud.

"You're so gross," she said.

"It's why you love me," he countered.

"I love you because you're going to tell me what I should do about Dad, so that he'll give Wade a chance and not go all Rapunzel on me and build a tower to lock me up in."

"I have no advice," he said, chuckling at his sister's analogy, not because it was outlandish, but because he could see his father going that far if anyone mentioned the option while within his earshot. "But it seems to me that following Wade's way isn't a bad start. Take it slow. You don't need to rush into anything at your age, especially when it comes to boys."

"Is that what ruined you and Allie?"

"Excuse me?"

"When you got hurt and then Allie lost the baby, you rushed to break up with her before you'd even left the hospital. Then she rushed off to school. Rush, rush, rush. I can see how it hasn't worked out too well for you."

James scowled at his sister, but she lifted her chin and met his disapproving gaze head-on. Damn if when the girl decided to add cement to her spine, she chose the quick-drying kind.

"I don't want to have this conversation with you," he muttered, taking away her soda bottle even though she wasn't done. He dumped the contents in the sink, rinsed the inside and threw the glass bottle into the bin beside the door.

She coolly slid her chair out, stalked to the fridge, pulled another cold one out and popped the top with a loud swoosh.

"Dad's right. You're a pain in the ass," he concluded.

"Dad's never said that and even if he had, I'd take it as a compliment. I'm tired of always doing what everyone else wants me to, James Hooker, and that includes you. Seems to me that you need someone to talk to. About Allie. About the past. About the fact that she spent the night here last night but now she's gone and maybe you're not sure if she's coming back."

"She's coming back," he insisted, though to be honest, he wasn't entirely confident she would. He couldn't help but think that once she got away, she'd realize what a mistake she'd make if she opted to stay in Lost Gun rather than take a job that would pay her to live at a five-star resort.

"I hope she does," Ginny went on. "She's a good person. I know she's been chasing you around for a long time, but maybe because she's just a gal who knows what she wants. I'm finding I appreciate that more lately. And I've always liked her anyway. She never bossed me around when I was a kid, even when you did. She's pretty and she's smart, and obviously you still have the hots for her. And let's face it, you're not getting any younger. I would like to be an aunt someday and like it or not, you're my only hope."

He crossed his arms over his chest and kicked one ankle atop the other as he leaned back on the counter, trying to look as if this conversation hadn't digressed into a topic he'd rather not be discussing with his teenage sister.

"So you think I should ask Allie to give up her plans and dreams for the future and come back home to give us another shot because you want to be an aunt?"

Ginny grinned. "It's as good a reason as any other. Except for maybe the fact that you still love her."

"Oh, I do? How the hell do you know what's inside my head?"

"Well, first of all, love doesn't exist in your head. If it did, no one would ever feel it because most of the time, it makes absolutely no sense. But if you didn't still love her, you would have ended things with her a long time ago."

"I did end things with her."

"Ha! You may have broken up with her, but you never really ended things. You've been stringing her along for years."

"Before last night, I barely talked to her."

"But you did talk to her. And when you did, you never once said, 'Allie, we have no chance of ever getting back together. I've moved on and you should, too,' did you?"

He frowned. No, he hadn't. Even when he was still angry and bitter, he could never bring himself to tear Allie apart more than he already had that day in the hospital when he'd said things he'd had no business saying out loud to the girl he'd once spent hours making love to—the same girl who'd lost his baby to a miscarriage.

"I didn't want to be cruel."

"You didn't want to lose her," his sister insisted. "Somewhere in the back of that thick head of yours, you wanted her back. You just weren't ready to face it. Now you are. So face it. Get her back if that's what you want or let her go for good, but stop stringing her along like a pull toy. That's cruel."

He pushed away from the counter and pulled open the back door. He had chores to do, more than he might be able to finish before Allie came back for dinner. But he supposed if he gave his sister's opinion a minute's worth of consideration, he wouldn't be able to argue with her reasoning.

But as much as he now wanted to figure out if he and Allie could make their relationship work again, how could he ask her to come back for good when coming home meant passing up a once-in-a-lifetime career opportunity in the Caribbean? He was tied down to landlocked Lost Gun, Texas. How could they ever make it work?

But if they didn't try, how many more years were they going to live as slaves to regret, fear and resentment?

"It's not that easy," he muttered before he whistled for the dogs to follow him out to the stables.

His sister jogged to catch up. "Love never is, big brother. Love never is."

ALLIE LAID HER CLOTHES across her bed, wondering why she hadn't packed her extra pair of skinny jeans. They'd look awesome with her pink blouse, the one with the frills that reminded her of the prom dress she'd worn on what had been her last big date with James. Shortly after that magical night, she'd realized that the nausea she'd been fighting off had not been a sign of the flu, but that she was pregnant—and thus had fallen the first domino in the chain that had thrown her life into chaos.

But now she had a chance to find her direction again. The years she and James had been apart had worked both for them and against them. Forgiveness now came easier—just as it was simpler now to forget all the angry words from so long ago, when they were both young and raw from the pain of losing so much.

Now, they were older. Wiser. Lonelier. And though Allie had fruitlessly tried to lure Hook back into her life over the years, absence must have finally made his heart grow fond enough for him to finally let her catch him. It certainly had elevated the heat between them. Her body still thrummed from their lovemaking. The entire outer layer of her skin tingled with anticipation of more kisses and more touches, while the deepest recess of her heart longed for the rare and intimate connection she could share with him and only him.

They had so much they could give each other, physically and emotionally. But first they had to make it through dinner.

She pawed through the outfits she'd stuffed into her suitcase, then decided she hadn't brought anything she liked. She turned to the closet her aunt had reserved for her the first time she'd come home from school. Over time, she'd forgotten various things or decided she no longer needed them—but her aunt had kept them all, in case a future need arose. Lost Gun had that effect on the people. You could move away, but you couldn't help but leave things behind that you'd need when you least expected it.

She giggled at the progression of her fashion history and made a mental note to pack up some of the more dated items for immediate disposal. The lime-green dress she'd been forced to wear for her father's wedding went to the top of that pile. She growled at the snug leather vest she remembered purchasing at a Western-themed store in Dallas that catered to girls who wanted to catch themselves a cowboy, then frowned when she realized she'd never worked up the guts to wear it in public. She tried it on, but without the woefully needed skinny jeans, she abandoned the idea. Besides, she was better off saving it for another time, when she wanted James to only have sex on his brain.

She loved how hot he still was for her, but she wanted tonight to be about more than lust. Attraction was all well and good, but now they needed to deal with the harder issues. He'd sunk every last dime into the J. Roger renovation and the business would keep him rooted in Lost Gun for the rest of his life. She, on the other hand, had chosen a career that couldn't be pursued in a town where the biggest body of water was a man-made lake twenty miles north.

She had decisions to make—and so did he.

But before she could make up her mind about her future, she had to know if the promises they'd made so long ago had survived.

She dug deeper in the closet, whistling when she found a pretty butter-yellow sundress that she couldn't remember if she'd ever worn. It was simple. Sexy, but not too sexy. Short skirt. Halter top. It reminded her of lazy days and sultry nights and dancing in the moonlight to music streaming from the AM radio in his pickup.

Deciding it was perfect, she swept her hair up into a loose ponytail, dabbed the perfume James liked best between her braless breasts and slipped her feet into the strappy, high-heeled sandals he'd seemed to like so much last night, though she hadn't had a chance to wear them. Maybe tonight wasn't going to be about sex, per se, but she knew they'd end up in bed. Whether it was to celebrate a new beginning or to seal their past for good had yet to be determined.

She grabbed her keys and the overnight bag she'd

stuffed with a change of clothes for tomorrow morning and the bottle of wine she'd promised—a hearty red to match the steak she had no doubt he'd be throwing on his grill—and headed down the back stairs, keeping herself out of sight of the customers in the diner. Crossing to the side alley where she'd parked her car, she was unlocking her door when she heard someone call her name.

Emerging from the diner's exit was the last man she expected ever to see in Lost Gun, Texas.

"Eric?" she said, nearly dropping her keys. "What are you doing here?"

Eric Rayburn, looking entirely out of place in a breezy Hawaiian shirt, loose khakis and deck shoes, grinned so that his white teeth shone in his perennially tanned face. "I've come to take you to paradise, Barrie. And don't try to put me off again. This time, I'm not taking no for an answer."

9

ALLIE COULDN'T BELIEVE this was happening. Okay, so she had ignored Eric's repeated phone messages and put Samantha's warning that her doctorate advisor was determined to track her down out of her mind. But she'd never expected the man to show up in Lost Gun.

"How did you find me?"

"Discovering the location of your hometown proved infinitely easier than tracking down your cell-phone number. One quick glance through your college records and here I am."

She frowned at the invasion of her privacy, but figured she'd brought this on herself. Eric Rayburn had been an exacting doctorate advisor and a challenging teacher. She couldn't have expected he'd wait forever for her answer to his more than generous offer—not to mention his hints that his interest in her was more than just professional.

"I was heading back to Port Aransas the day after tomorrow. You would have gotten your answer then."

"Did you tell me that? Did you pass that message along via Samantha? Your dissertation, I happen to know, just needs a little tweaking and the committee doesn't meet for a couple of more weeks. As far as I knew, you'd gone home for an extended leave."

He slipped his hands into his pockets, his casual attire entirely out of place in her decidedly Western hometown. She was half expecting some kind of chemical reaction as the two worlds she'd tried so hard to keep separate and distinct clashed together, but the most that happened was an eruption of sweat over her lower lip and between her breasts. It was warm out tonight and the shock of seeing Eric standing one block off Lost Gun's main street made her dizzy.

"I guess I didn't. I'm sorry. But why the rush? The job doesn't start until the fall."

"Thanks to a mild hurricane season," he said, "the resort construction is months ahead of schedule. Management wants my team in the water in three weeks to start collecting specimens. They want the place teeming with sea creatures before the bigwig celebrities fly out to check on the progress of their private bungalows. Sales haven't been as robust as they'd hoped and they need us to sweeten the pot."

Allie found herself shaking her head, though she wasn't sure if it was Eric's timing that had her thinking, *No, no, no,* or the final realization that her desire to fly out to the Caribbean and work on an exciting private-sector job was nothing compared to her need to drive out to the J. Roger and figure out if she and James had anything left to salvage.

"I can't," she said.

"Don't be ridiculous, Allie," Eric said. "This is the kind of job that marine biologists dream about. What are you going to do if you pass this up?"

"I meant, I can't deal with this right now, Eric. I have some place I need to be."

"Yes, and it's in the islands with me."

She pulled the part of her brain that was already on the way to the J. Roger back into her head. She looked at Eric again, this time with her full gaze, and the sudden intensity in his dark eyes struck her hard.

"I'm sure you don't mean that the way it sounds," she said.

"You need to open your eyes to reality, Allie. I've seen your town. Took me all of fifteen minutes. What could there possibly be for you here? You're better than Lost Gun, Texas, and you are definitely too good for a man who doesn't know a great thing when he has it."

She staggered a few steps backward, knocked unsteady not only by his words, but the presumptuousness of him saying them out loud.

She'd known Eric Rayburn for four years. He'd been her doctorate advisor for two and not once had he pried into her personal life, though she supposed that the closed quarters of their research vessels might have meant he'd overheard more of her conversations with Samantha than she'd ever intended.

"You don't know what you're talking about," she said.

"No, you're right. I don't. I only know what I see, which is a beautiful, sexy, intelligent woman who spends every free moment she has running back to her hometown to try and win back a man who threw her away a long time ago."

If possible, her temperature rose another ten degrees.

"That's none of your business."

"Maybe," he conceded, "but I care about you. You can't let old feelings keep you from following your dreams—and trust me, I know what I'm talking about. You've got to put the past behind you and embrace the future. I thought I was going to teach college for the rest of my life and live a peaceful existence doing what I loved. But now I have a chance to do something new and unexpected. I want to take you with me. You just have to say yes."

Allie didn't flinch when Eric grabbed her wrists. His touch wasn't gentle, but it wasn't rough, either. It was desperate. Passionate. Seeing how much the job at the resort meant to him clarified so much for her—it was as if her eyes were opening for the first time.

She'd never wanted anything as badly—nothing, except James and a life in Lost Gun.

She worked her hands out of his. "I can't say yes."

"God, Allie. You're passing up a once-in-a-lifetime opportunity. And not just for your career, either. Look, I—"

She held her hand up, stopping him before he said more than necessary.

"I've loved the university, Eric. I've loved every project, every exam, every long, hot day in the Gulf when we were lucky to find one decent specimen. But I don't have to use that knowledge only one way. I can teach. Inspire the kids like me who've been landlocked all their lives. But I can't go to the Caribbean," she said.

"You can, Allie. Your talents would be wasted here."

She patted his cheek. "You know that's not true."

"So it's me you don't want."

She frowned, not wanting to say what needed to be said. He was truly a breathtaking man. Intelligent, dedicated, handsome. But she'd never truly noticed because her heart had always—and would always—belong to James Hooker.

"You're a great guy, Eric. An amazing teacher and an attractive man, but my heart is here in Lost Gun, with the man I've loved since I was fourteen. Maybe it sounds ridiculous to anyone else, but it makes perfect sense to me. In fact, now that he's let me back into his life, my whole life makes sense. The resort job is once-in-a-lifetime. But so is falling in love with your soul mate."

"I hope to hell you're talking about me."

Allie jumped at the sound of James's voice echoing from across the alley. A thrill ran through her at the sight of him standing so rigid and strong, his eyes blazing with clear and intense jealousy.

"For Pete's sake," she said, stepping back out of Eric's personal space and slamming her fists onto her hips, "who the hell else would I be talking about?"

She could see his scowl threatening to turn into a grin. Unwilling to wait, she marched across the street, slapped her hands on either side of his face and tugged him down for a kiss—a possessive, make-no-mistakes, you're-the-only-man-for-me kiss that came from the depth of her soul and made her toes curl inside her sexy, sassy sandals.

When James wrapped his arms around her and lifted her off the ground, she knew they'd come one step closer to finally breaking down the last barrier.

He set her down, his arms still wrapped around her, which was good because she was pretty sure that otherwise, she would have toppled right off her four-inch heels.

From behind them, Eric cleared his throat.

After exchanging an embarrassed look with James, she twisted around in his arms, then locked her hands over his, which he had crossed possessively over her midsection.

"I'm sorry, Eric," she said to him from across the alley. "I've made my decision."

Eric clucked his tongue and toed the ground with his deck shoes, but she could tell by the smile in his eyes that he wasn't surprised. He'd taken a chance and it hadn't worked out. With his laissez-faire attitude, he'd recover, if he hadn't already.

"The team would have been stronger with you as a player, Allie, but I see you've made up your mind. At least, now I know. Will you be coming back to Port Aransas to present your dissertation?"

"I didn't work all these years not to finish my doctorate. I'll be back on Monday. But after the review committee makes their decision, I'm coming back home." She threw an uncertain glance over her shoulder. "No matter what happens, I'm coming home."

Nodding, Eric crossed the road, held his hand out to James, who released Allie halfway, just enough to force his damaged right hand into Eric's and give what she imagined must have been a painful shake. But in true cowboy fashion, he didn't wince or flinch, though his left hand did squeeze her a little tighter around the middle.

"You're a lucky man," Eric said.

"I don't need a college professor to tell me that," Hook answered.

Eric smirked. "Don't you?"

Before Hook could argue, Eric let go of his hand and addressed Allie. "I'll see you back at the Institute."

Without a backward glance, he used the diner's back door to return the way he'd come.

Allie turned around and pressed her cheek to James's chest. She could hear his heart slamming against his ribs, but even as his beat double-time, hers had slowed to an even, comfortable cadence. After what seemed like a lifetime of uncertainty, she'd made her choice. No matter what happened between her and James, it felt right.

More than right. It felt like heaven.

He pushed her back, but only enough for him to be able to look her in the eye. "So let me get this straight— you're giving up that job for me?"

In the uncertain light from the streetlamp, his gaze was hard to read.

Hard, but not impossible. Her stomach suddenly dipped with the weight of her choice.

"You don't think I should?" she asked.

"It's your choice," he replied. "But before that guy leaves town, I think you need to know the truth about me. The whole truth. And it isn't going to be pretty."

HOLDING HER SO CLOSE, James was sure Allie could hear his heart thudding against his chest like a grandfather clock on steroids. Maylene's phone call had caught him completely off-guard. He hadn't fully understood how much he'd been counting on Allie's return to the ranch until he'd been faced with even the smallest possibility that she might stand him up.

After years of her chasing him, he'd hopped into his truck and broke every speed limit in the county to reach town before the man who was offering Allie a life in paradise beat him to the punch and stopped him from offering her the world.

Well, maybe not the whole world—but his world— one that would be worth much if she wasn't the center of it.

"There's nothing you can tell me about you that I don't already know," she assured him.

He held her tighter again, suddenly reluctant to fill in the gaps in their history that could end up derailing all the progress they'd made over the past two days. But she deserved to know everything. Only then could she make the right choice.

"I wish that were true. Fact is, you might want to ask that prof of yours for a little more time before you make your decision about going to the islands."

"I don't understand," she said. "You want me to take the job?"

"No way in hell," he replied.

She laughed. "Well, then, you're not making any sense. I know everything there is to know about you. I've practically been your stalker, remember?"

He laughed, tugged her forward and kissed the top of her head. God, he wished it could all be that easy, but what good things in life ever were?

"Look, I promised your Aunt Maylene that I wouldn't stick my nose into your career aspirations, and pissing her off isn't a particularly good idea. No telling what she'll put into my pie."

"Oh, God! I forgot the pie!"

"I know," he grinned, tugging her back close. He didn't know what she was wearing under this sweet little yellow dress, but he didn't imagine it was much, judging by the way her ample breasts pressed soft, full and unbound against his chest. He had a strong inclination to hold her here for a while, maybe see just how much room she had in the backseat of her car. "That's why I came out here to get you."

"Boy, you really wanted that pie."

"What I really wanted was you," he confessed. "Maylene called. She said you'd already left and that you'd forgotten our dessert, but I think that was just a cover for letting me know that some beach-bum professor from the coast had just driven into town looking for you, more than likely to try and influence you into taking off with him to that fancy island instead of making good on our date. I guess she decided I deserved a chance to talk you into turning it down."

"And I beat you to it," she said.

He tried to ferret out any sound of regret in her voice, but he didn't hear anything but irony. And maybe, if he was honest with himself, relief.

"I want you to make the right decision, Allie. I don't want you to have any regrets. And for that, you need to know the whole story of why I pushed you away."

God knew he didn't want her to change her whole life only for things not to work out between them. On the other hand, he wanted a chance to try. And he couldn't do that if she lived hundreds of miles away.

"I don't mean to damage your ego or anything, Hook, but I said no for me just as much as I did for you. But if you have something to say, say it."

"Not here."

She retrieved her bag from where she'd dropped it, shrugged it over her shoulder and then hooked her arm in his. "Lead the way."

10

"YOU DON'T WANT TO DRIVE your own car out to the ranch so the whole of Lost Gun doesn't know whose bed you're going to be in tonight?" he asked, still hopeful that things would end well with Allie and not with her demanding he take her immediately back to town after vowing to never speak to him again.

Blissfully unaware of what he intended to tell her, she tugged him forward and placed a promissory kiss on his chin. "I don't give a damn about what people know if you don't. Besides, I've been wanting a ride in that big truck of yours for a long time. If it's anything like that old pickup you had back in school, I remember the front cab being rather roomy."

He chuckled. "It is the old pickup from high school. You just don't recognize it under all the dents and faded paint."

She leaned in closer to him, her eyes twinkling with wicked intentions. "Good. Then I'm on familiar territory."

His abdomen tightened as he led her around to where he'd parked in front of the hardware store beside the diner. An unfamiliar convertible not unlike Allie's, though a much newer model and sparkling with bright red paint, was parked a couple of cars over. The professor was still inside. As much as James had been craving Maylene's lemon-meringue pie and had plans for how he wanted to share dessert with the woman beside him, he craved Allie a hell of a lot more. Without a word, he opened the passenger-side door and handed Allie into the cab.

As he hit the highway, she turned up the radio, then scooted over close and locked her small fingers with his damaged ones, her gaze alternating between watching the road and stealing increasingly heated glances.

He remembered the things he used to coax her into doing to him while he was driving his truck. From the combustible glow in her emerald eyes, she hadn't forgotten, either. One word from him, one shift of his body to give her easy access and he'd be fighting to keep his focus as he traversed the country roads.

But as much as he'd love to feel her hot palm around his rigid sex, the thought of what he had to say to her first kept him cool. There'd be time for that soon. If she listened. If she forgave him.

When he nearly spun out taking the curve around the back of the ranch house, she squealed and braced her hands on the dashboard. By the time he braked, she was flushed and a little out of breath.

"You don't have to be in such a hurry," she said. "I'm not going anywhere, remember?"

He hopped out of the truck. "You don't know that, yet. I can't offer you paradise, Allie."

"Can't you?" she asked. Still in the cab, she slipped her arms around his neck and teased her fingers in his hair.

He reached deep down and pulled out the largest

chunk of self-control he had in him. He had all night to show Allie the kind of paradise he could promise, but not until she knew the whole truth.

"I was really pissed at you," he admitted.

That cooled her jets. She sat back and tilted her head to the side. "When I was talking to Eric?"

"Who? No. I mean, who can blame the guy for wanting to see you in a bikini every day?"

"He's seen me in a bikini every day for years. We don't exactly wear lab coats on our research vessels. He's a good guy, but he's not the guy for me. You are."

He wanted to kiss her. He wanted to touch her. He wanted to thank her for choosing him over paradise by making love to her until neither one of them could think or speak or breathe. But first, he had to make sure she'd made the right decision.

"I wasn't talking about him. When you lost the baby. I was screwed up, you know that. The meds, the pain, the fact that I wasn't going to be able to bull ride again. Hell, with a bum hand, I wasn't sure what I'd be able to do. I was angry."

"You had every right to be. Your whole future had just imploded."

"I was angry at *you*."

She folded her lips together and though her chin quivered for a second, she kept a tight hold on her composure. Lord, she had a tough hide—tougher than he'd ever given her credit for.

"I shouldn't have told you about being pregnant right before you got on the bull," she repeated. "I've said I was sorry—"

"That's not what I was angry about. I know you thought that's why I wouldn't let you back in my life, but that wasn't the real reason."

He yanked his hat off, tossed it in the back of the truck and jabbed his fingers through his hair. God, this sucked. But he couldn't keep it in anymore.

After his talk with Ginny this afternoon, he'd decided that the only way he and Allie could really make a go at a relationship was to be completely honest and up-front about all that had happened between them. He knew Allie had poured her heart out and he knew her regrets had been genuine. She'd been trying to atone for a long time—but he'd been holding back.

She scooted out of the truck behind him, the heels of her spiky shoes digging into the dirt. "What are you trying to tell me?"

He took a deep breath, then pushed out the words.

"The baby. I was angry about the baby. I thought you lost the baby because you didn't really want it in the first place. And then you took off so fast for college, I figured you couldn't get away from me fast enough. As if you'd dodged a bullet."

As he'd expected, as he'd dreaded, her face fell. She turned away, but he jogged around her so she'd have to face him—him and his cruelest weakness.

"I know now that it was stupid," he said. "Losing the baby must have killed you the same way it killed me and when I pushed you away, you just threw yourself into school to keep sane. I get it now. It took a long time for my good sense to kick back in. But by then, I felt like such an idiot, I couldn't face this moment, telling you why I wouldn't let you close again for so long."

"Then why are telling me this now?"

Her voice had a bite of rage, which he deserved. It was bad enough that she'd spent the last nine years thinking he blamed her for the injury to his hand, but adding to it that he'd thought she'd lost the baby on purpose was a hard truth to bear. But he couldn't make excuses or pretend his anger toward her was at all reasonable or justified. If they were going to make a run at a real reunion, they had to start with a totally clean slate—or at least, they had to clear out all the ugly anger, resentment and sadness.

"I was wrong. I was a fool. I was stupid and mean and self-centered."

He took a step forward and he was shocked that she didn't push him away. Though her eyes were wary, she allowed him close enough to crook his finger beneath her chin, and she turned her face up to his.

"Before you turn down a dream job on a tropical island, you need to know what kind of first-class idiot you'll be getting instead. I'm fully aware of my stupidity and I have every intention of spending the rest of my life proving that I've gotten a lot smarter since then. And I love you. I've always loved you."

She shook her head and he took this as a sign to back away. As much as he desperately wanted to wrap her up in his arms and squeeze the anguish out of her, he couldn't. She had to come to terms with it on her own.

After several long, torturous minutes, she held out her palm.

"Keys?"

She wanted to leave? Of course, she did. He dug into his pocket, trying to squelch the image of her tearing back to town and finding her professor and not only taking the job, but using the man for angry revenge sex that would make her more miserable than he was.

But he didn't have the right to stop her. He handed her the keys and she climbed into the driver's seat. She slammed the door and started up the engine, but she didn't leave.

Through the window, he watched her brace her hands on the steering wheel as if she was doing ninety around a treacherous bend rather than sitting still behind his house. Her lips moved and without being able to hear a word, knew she was cursing a blue streak. He stepped closer, his heart aching. God, he hoped she wasn't crying. He'd caused her enough tears. Even on his best behavior, he'd never make up for what he'd put her through, then or now.

She fumbled around the cab as if looking for the gear, but finally, she rolled down the window.

"Well?"

He stepped even closer, half-afraid she was waiting for him to get his feet under the wheels so she could run them over.

"Well, what?"

She looked at him as if he was the most idiotic man on the planet.

"What are you waiting for? Get in the damned truck."

He wasn't about to argue. If there was one thing he'd learned over the past nine years, it was that when Allie Barrie set her mind to something, he was better off just giving in and going along for the ride.

ALLIE WAS HURT. How could he have thought so little of her? Knowing that he'd thought, even if only in his weakest moment, that she'd been glad about the miscarriage, tore at her insides like a great white on a feeding frenzy. Once she'd moved away from Lost Gun and had thrown herself into school, there had been moments— short, shameful moments—when she'd been thankful she didn't have to face a future as a single mother.

But not even those selfish thoughts had diminished the ache she'd felt for that lost child. The lost future.

Nothing except time. Distance. Maybe a little wisdom. They'd both been young. They'd both made mistakes. They'd both been unprepared to handle the instantaneous deconstruction of the relationship they'd immersed themselves in for four blissful years when their disagreements had been over nothing more than which movie to go see on the weekend or who should say goodbye first when they ended one of their late-night phone calls. When real trouble had brewed, they'd faltered. Failed.

And yet, that was then—this was now. Growing up had meant accepting the fallibility of her choices and the inevitability of pain. Didn't tragedy make triumph so much sweeter? As much as she thought she should conjure up a lot more hurt over what James had just told her, the longer she drove, the more her sadness waned. The past was the past. And with the future she'd fought for so close at hand, she simply couldn't muster up the energy to stay mad.

How could she, when she loved him so completely?

"So, where are we headed?" he asked once she made a turn that revealed that she wasn't going back to town.

She kept her smile small. "You don't recognize the route?"

Truth was, he hadn't been watching the road. From the moment he'd jumped into the cab beside her, his gaze hadn't left her. Now, he took a second to mark their location and once he put two and two together, his grin matched hers.

Though she was surprised she could traverse this path in the dark after all these years, she was proud of herself when the headlights flashed over the rock formation that marked the first landmark on the path to their secret spot. The truck hopped and jostled over the uneven terrain, but even as James braced his hands on the dash to keep from bumping his head, she watched his face transform from self-recrimination to hopeful uncertainty to sheer anticipation.

She slowed down as they approached the curtain of branches that would lead them to their destination. Just beyond the trees that would hide them from the world, she eased the truck to a stop and shut off the ignition, though she left the battery going so that the lights cast thick beams of white over the little meadow where they'd first made love.

"It's changed," she said, peering through the windshield.

He reached around the back and pulled out an old, tattered blanket—one, she suspected, he'd stored there since before she left town. "Not that much."

He was out and opening her door before she could wonder how many times he'd brought other women out here.

Luckily, he allayed her fears by adding, "Sometimes when I'm out riding fences, I drop on by, see if the creek has dried up or if the blackberry bush is still giving up fruit."

She took his hand and slid down beside him. "Is it?"

His grin was unstoppable. She hadn't said as much, but he knew she forgave him, just as he had obviously forgiven her. What they'd felt back then didn't matter anymore—not when what they felt now was so much better.

"They're not as sweet, but maybe that's because I wasn't sharing them with you."

Allie locked her arms around his neck and pulled

herself up high enough to kiss him. The pressing of lips was at first soft and sensuous, brimming with the absolution they both had so desperately needed, but no longer had to give. But in the span of a heartbeat, he buoyed his hands beneath her bottom and tugged her hard against him, changing the mood instantly to one of hot desire and wanton desperation. She let him lift her high, wrapping her legs tight around his waist in her final act of surrender.

He was what she wanted—what she'd always wanted.

He broke away, his eyes wide. "You're not wearing panties."

She grinned wickedly. "Remember the last time we came out here and I wasn't wearing any panties?"

He growled, even as he slipped his hands fully under her skirt and carried her into the wash of light. The feel of his palms, rough and scarred, sparked each and every nerve ending in her body. Her sex throbbed for him. Her nipples ached. Her legs shook as he set her down long enough to throw the blanket haphazardly over the ground before he lifted her again and placed her down on the frayed wool as if she were a china doll rather than a living, breathing, writhing woman.

She unhooked her top, lowering the material as he knelt between her legs.

"You're so beautiful," he crooned. He lifted her skirt. "All of you."

He ran his hands down her thighs. She snagged her bottom lip in her teeth as he eased her knees farther apart, then leaned down and kissed her mouth with exquisite gentleness.

"I love you, Allie. I always have."

"I never stopped loving you," she replied. "Not for a minute."

"I was a fool."

"But you're not now," she added.

"No, ma'am, I'm not now. I'm the luckiest man in the world. And to show you my appreciation, I'm going to make love to you all night long."

She speared her hands into his hair and ran her thumbs over his brows, nearly drowning in the depths of his Caribbean-blue eyes. That was all she needed of that part of the world—the color. And now she could experience the hypnotic sapphire experience right here in Lost Gun.

"I was hoping for more than just all night," she admitted.

He grinned even as he retrieved a condom from his wallet, tore out of his shirt and discarded his belt. "How about a lifetime?"

She unbuttoned his jeans and slowly, torturously, worked the zipper down over his rigid erection. "I think that's a good place to start."

Seconds later, they were nearly naked. Minutes later, she was lost in the throes of pure and unadulterated pleasure. By the end of the hour, she had him trapped underneath her while she milked his body for the orgasm she so desperately needed and the closeness she'd never dreamed they'd share again, not for more than a weekend.

And yet, now she felt certain they'd be together until the end of time.

When she collapsed, spent against his chest, her dress tangled around her waist, he chased away the last of her chills by running his hand rhythmically up and down her spine. By the texture and level of pressure, she knew that his touch would always bring her an intense and unstoppable sense of safety. The bull had

crushed his career with its cruel and uncaring hooves—
but he hadn't stopped Hook's ability to love her one iota.

"We're going to have to walk back to the ranch house
if we let that battery run much longer," she said.

He chuckled, the movement reminding her that he
was still inside her, still hard, still needful and still
hers to love.

"I'm not quite ready for you to get up just yet," he
said.

She swiveled her hips, eliciting a torturous groan
from deep in the back of his throat. "You're the one
holding out this time."

Per usual, she'd taken a while to reach her apex, but
no matter how she'd tried, he'd resisted toppling over
with her. Not that she minded. She'd always been on
the receiving end of his patient and determined attention. Maybe it was time to return the favor—even if it
took all night. And tomorrow. And the next day. And
the next day. And the next….

"I just don't want this to end," he confessed, grasping her hips and guiding her undulations slightly to the
left. He moaned when they reached the right spot, an
angle that allowed him slightly deeper access.

"This night or us?" she asked. Her body, though
spent, tingled to life again.

She tucked her knees under her and arched her back
until he dug his fingers into her flesh and croaked out
a torturous, "Both."

"Then both, cowboy, is what you're going to get."

* * * * *

#705 NORTHERN RENEGADE
Alaskan Heat
Jennifer LaBrecque
Former Gunnery Sergeant Liam Reinhardt thinks he's fought his last battle when he rolls into the small town of Good Riddance, Alaska, on the back of his motorcycle. Then he meets Tansy Wellington....

#706 JUST ONE NIGHT
The Wrong Bed
Nancy Warren
Realtor Hailey Fleming is surprised to find a sexy stranger fast asleep in the house she's just listed. Rob Klassen is floored—his house *isn't* for sale—and convincing Hailey of that *and* his good intentions might keep them up all night!

#707 THE MIGHTY QUINNS: KIERAN
The Mighty Quinns
Kate Hoffmann
When Kieran Quinn comes to the rescue of a beautiful blonde, all he expects is a thank-you. But runaway country star Maddie West is on a quest to find herself. And Kieran, with his sexy good looks and killer smile, is the perfect traveling companion.

#708 FULL SURRENDER
Uniformly Hot!
Joanne Rock
Photographer Stephanie Rosen really needs to get her mojo back. And who better for the job than the guy who rocked her world five years ago, navy lieutenant Daniel Murphy?

#709 UNDONE BY MOONLIGHT
Flirting with Justice
Wendy Etherington
As Calla Tucker uncovers the truth about her detective friend Devin Antonio's suspension, more secrets are revealed, including their long, secret attraction for each other....

#710 WATCH ME
Stepping Up
Lisa Renee Jones
A "curse" has hit TV's hottest reality dance show and security chief Sam Kellar is trying to keep control. What he can't control, though, is his desire for Meagan Tippan, the show's creator!

You can find more information on upcoming Harlequin® titles, free excerpts and more at www.Harlequin.com.

HBCNM0812

REQUEST YOUR FREE BOOKS!
2 FREE NOVELS PLUS 2 FREE GIFTS!

Harlequin® *Blaze*™

red-hot reads!

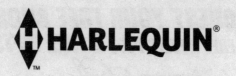

HARLEQUIN®

SO YOU THINK YOU CAN WRITE

Harlequin and Mills & Boon are joining forces in a global search for new authors.

In September 2012 we're launching our biggest contest yet—with the prize of being published by the world's leader in romance fiction!

Look for more information on our website, **www.soyouthinkyoucanwrite.com**

So you think you can write? Show us!

Enjoy this sneak peek of USA TODAY *bestselling author*
Maureen Child's newest title
UP CLOSE AND PERSONAL

Available September 2012 from Harlequin® Desire!

"**L**aura, I know you're in there!"

Ronan Connolly pounded on the bright blue front door, then paused to listen. Not a sound from inside the house, though he knew too well that Laura was in there. Hell, he could practically *feel* her standing just on the other side of the damned door.

He glanced at her car parked alongside the house, then glared again at the still-closed front door.

"You won't convince me you're not at home. Your car is parked in the street, Laura."

Her voice came then, muffled but clear. "It's a driveway in America, Ronan. You're not in Ireland, remember?"

"More's the pity." He scrubbed one hand across his face and rolled his eyes in frustration. If they were in Ireland right now, he'd have half the village of Dunley on his side and he'd bloody well get her to open the door.

"I heard that," she said.

Grinding his teeth together, he counted to ten. Then did it a second time. "Whatever the hell you want to call it, Laura, your car is *here* and so are you. Why not open the door and we can talk this out. Together. In private."

"I've got nothing to say to you."

He laughed shortly. That would be a first indeed, he told himself. A more opinionated woman he had never met. He had to admit, he had enjoyed verbally sparring with her. He admired a quick mind and a sharp tongue. He'd admired her even more once he'd gotten her into his bed.

He glanced down at the dozen red roses he held clutched in his right hand and called himself a damned fool for thinking this woman would be swayed by pretty flowers and a smooth speech. Hell, she hadn't even *seen* the flowers yet. At this rate, she never would.

Huffing out an impatient breath, he lowered his voice. "You know why I'm here. Let's get it done and have it over then."

There was a moment's pause, as if she were thinking about what he'd said. Then she spoke up again. "You can't have him."

"What?"

"You heard me."

Ronan narrowed his gaze fiercely on the door as if he could see through the panel to the woman beyond. "Aye, I heard you. Though, I don't believe it. I've come for what's mine, Laura, and I'm not leaving until I have it."

Will Ronan get what he's come for?

Find out in Maureen Child's new title
UP CLOSE AND PERSONAL

Available September 2012 from Harlequin® Desire!